THE FORTUNES OF TEXAS

*Follow the lives and loves of a complex family
with a rich history and deep ties
in the Lone Star State*

HITTING THE JACKPOT

The Maloneys of Chatelaine, Texas,
have just discovered they are blood relations
to the Fortunes—which makes them instant
millionaires. But their inheritance comes
with a big secret attached that could change
everything for their small-town family...

Flush with new money, Max Fortune Maloney is
hoping real estate agent Eliza Henry can help
him find the perfect home. And she quickly
does—but it's complicated. When they have
to "play house" to make the sale, committed
bachelor Max realizes he likes his fake girlfriend
a little too much for comfort...

Dear Reader,

Welcome to Chatelaine, Texas, or if you have been here before, welcome back!

In *Fortune's Dream House*, Max Fortune Maloney is a newly minted millionaire. Eliza Henry is the real estate agent helping him find his dream home. A visit to a castle, a charity bachelor auction and a fake relationship unexpectedly bring them closer.

But Max is skeptical about relationships. Eliza believes two people can build a life together. Finding common ground requires them to let go of their fears, embrace childhood dreams and disappointments, and trust in the possibility of love. What a journey! But the challenges are worth it.

I'd love to hear from you. Visit me at ninacrespo.com. Say hello and connect with me on Facebook, Instagram or sign up for my newsletter. There, I share about my books, upcoming appearances and my favorite things.

Thank you for choosing *Fortune's Dream House* as your new romance read. I hope you enjoy your book escape with Max and Eliza.

Wishing you all the best,

Nina

Fortune's Dream House

———

NINA CRESPO

HARLEQUIN

SPECIAL
EDITION

Special thanks and acknowledgment are given to
Nina Crespo for her contribution to
The Fortunes of Texas: Hitting the Jackpot miniseries.

HARLEQUIN®

SPECIAL EDITION™

Recycling programs
for this product may
not exist in your area.

ISBN-13: 978-1-335-72443-4

Fortune's Dream House

Copyright © 2023 by Harlequin Enterprises ULC

For questions and comments about the quality of this book,
please contact us at CustomerService@Harlequin.com.

Harlequin Enterprises ULC
22 Adelaide St. West, 41st Floor
Toronto, Ontario M5H 4E3, Canada
www.Harlequin.com

Printed in U.S.A.

Nina Crespo lives in Florida, where she indulges in her favorite passions—the beach, a good glass of wine, date night with her own real-life hero and dancing. Her lifelong addiction to romance began in her teens while on a "borrowing spree" in her older sister's bedroom, where she discovered her first romance novel. Let Nina's sensual contemporary stories feed your own addiction for love, romance and happily-ever-after. Visit her at ninacrespo.com.

Books by Nina Crespo

Harlequin Special Edition

Tillbridge Stables

The Cowboy's Claim
Her Sweet Temptation
The Cowgirl's Surprise Match

The Fortunes of Texas: The Hotel Fortune

An Officer and a Fortune

Small Town Secrets

A Chef's Kiss
The Designer's Secret

The Fortunes of Texas: Hitting the Jackpot

Fortune's Dream House

Visit the Author Profile page
at Harlequin.com for more titles.

To my real-life hero and best friend,
thank you for all you do. Cathy, your encouragement
is valuable beyond words. Michelle Major,
Heatherly Bell, Makenna Lee, Judy Duarte
and Allison Leigh, it's a pleasure to be a part of this
series with you. Susan Litman and Megan Broderick,
I so appreciate your patience and support.
And a huge thank-you to all of my readers.
May this book provide an enjoyable escape
that causes you to smile as you turn the pages.

Chapter One

The Chatelaine Report: No one would have guessed that GreatStore manager Linc Maloney would turn out to be the mastermind behind last month's epic New Year's bash at the LC Club on Lake Chatelaine! Now we have learned that his true name is Linc Fortune *Maloney and he is a suddenly a very rich man. But what's his secret? How did Linc come into all this money? And why won't he share with the rest of us? All kidding aside, we are investigating a lead that suggests Linc may not be the only new millionaire in town...*

Eliza Henry entered the corner restaurant near a strip of small shops outside San Antonio. As the door closed, a chilly breeze blew over her, and she hurried into the cozy lobby, grateful for the warmth in the wood-floored space.

After spending the past three days sitting in a hotel conference room downtown, fresh air, sunshine and the less crowded street had lured her out of her car without a coat. While the white blouse, black cardigan, jeans and boots she wore were a great fashion statement, they weren't a match for the chilly February weather. Still, she'd enjoyed the chance to stretch her legs.

She was looking forward to Sunday brunch with her friend Tess Lawford, but during the short walk to the restaurant, she'd envisioned the fields near her home dotted with mesquite and oak trees covered by an endless canopy of blue sky.

Some viewed Chatelaine as a small dusty town where time stood still. She saw it as a place where potential and progress would meet up someday. And she would be there, welcoming the excitement of change.

Eliza peeked from the lobby into the brightly lit dining area with blue chairs, wood tables, and green plants draping from colorful pots built into the walls. Spotting her auburn-haired friend of over five years seated at a four-top, she returned Tess's wave and walked in.

The chime of a familiar ringtone brought her to a halt.

Sharon, the office manager for Vale Real Estate Group, knew she was out of town. If she was calling her now, it must be important.

Eliza stepped back into the lobby and answered her phone. As she smoothed her dark, shoulder-length hair behind her ear, her silver-and-turquoise earring grazed her tawny-brown cheek. "Hi, Sharon."

"Hello, Eliza. Sorry to bother you, but I thought you

would want to know, Max Fortune Maloney called to stop the paperwork. He's decided not to put in an offer for the house on Sandview after all."

"What? He backed out again?"

A few weeks ago, Max had shown up at the Chatelaine real estate office where she worked as an agent requesting the moon and the stars—a large house with a swimming pool, a basketball court and a horse barn. Not an easy ask considering new homes hadn't been built in Chatelaine since ranchers had flocked there in the eighties, happy to have large pastures for grazing cattle.

But she'd risen to the challenge and come close to giving him the moon…three times.

First, she'd found him a two-story house with plenty of room to build everything he'd wanted. He'd claimed he was interested in the place, but he didn't get back to her in time with a bid and someone else had scooped it up. A week after that, Max had made an offer on a sprawling ranch-style home she'd shown him near Lake Chatelaine that had a large, premium stable and acres of land. He'd rescinded it the next day.

But out of all the properties she'd shown him so far, the house on Sandview Road that they'd looked at before she'd left for the conference had come the closest to his dream home. It wasn't officially on the market yet, and she had called in a favor for them to see the place before anyone else.

The property didn't have a horse barn, but it did have a pool and his unicorn-level requirement—a full-size basketball court. The owners had built it for their son who'd been a high school basketball star destined for bigger athletic opportunities in college.

As Eliza recalled the way Max's blue eyes had lit up when he'd walked into the air-conditioned, indoor court, confusion pushed out a breath. "Did he say why he changed his mind?"

"Not really. He just said he needed to take a pass."

"Well, I guess that's it, then. Thanks for the update."

"No problem. Sorry I didn't have better news. When you get a chance, check your schedule. I just added meetings with prospective buyers tomorrow morning and afternoon. And the open house on Fox Creek Trail has been moved to Tuesday. You had that one down as a possibility for Max along with other places near that area. Would you like for me to see if he's free that day?"

"No. I've decided not to take him to that open house after all. I don't think that property will suit his needs. I'll contact him myself about setting up a time to view other houses."

"Okay. If anything else changes, I'll update your schedule. And Eliza…about Max. He really did sound disappointed about declining to put an offer on the house."

"That's good to know. Thanks, Sharon. I'll see you tomorrow." Eliza put her phone away.

She appreciated Sharon's take on Max's situation, but his behavior was bizarre. Take a pass? What did that mean? The other times Max had walked away from an offer, she'd empathized with him and given him the benefit of the doubt. It wasn't uncommon for first-time home buyers to feel enthusiastic while viewing a house only to have second thoughts about it later. But now, his indecision was creeping toward the dreaded level of a difficult client.

Maybe he wasn't ready for home ownership. If that was the issue, she was fine with that. She just needed him to be clear about his intentions.

Dismissing the frustrating news, Eliza switched her focus to having some much-needed girl-time with her friend.

Inside the dining room, Tess stood as she reached the table. She was dressed in a camel-colored pantsuit, and the nude stiletto-heel pumps Tess wore added at least another three inches to her runway model height.

Tess beamed a huge smile and a hint of rosiness flushed in her cheeks. "Hey you." She came in for a hug.

"Hi." Eliza returned her friend's tight embrace.

After hanging her purse on the back of the chair, Eliza sat down and spread the cloth napkin folded in front of her on her lap. "Sorry I kept you waiting. I got a call from the office."

"No need to apologize. I'm just glad we were able to do this. A year is way too long for us not to get together in person."

"I know. Phone calls just aren't the same. I missed seeing you at the conference."

"I tried to pop in, but my schedule was insane. At least my new people got a chance to attend."

Two years ago, Tess had gone out on her own as a Realtor. She'd established herself in San Antonio and was now leading a team.

"How many agents are working for you?"

"Five, but I'm hiring more. New subdivisions and developments are going up, and I want us to be prepared to handle the expansion."

"That sounds exciting."

"It is."

They paused as a dark-haired server poured coffee, dropped off a basket of warm mini sweet rolls and pastries, and assured them she'd return to take their orders.

Tess snagged a Danish. "What about you? Things must be jumping in Chatelaine if you're receiving calls from the office on a Sunday."

"Jumping?" Eliza laughed. "No, not quite. And that call I just received wasn't good news. One of my clients backed out on making an offer on a house. Again."

"Again? How many times have they done it?"

"This makes three." Eliza put a glazed cinnamon roll on her plate. "Every time he expressed interest in a home, he seemed serious about it. I honestly don't know why he keeps changing his mind."

"Is there a significant other pulling the strings?"

"He's single. And there's no significant other that I know of."

"Is he cute?"

As Eliza sucked a drop of glaze from her thumb, a vision of blond-haired, blue-eyed Max came into her mind. He usually dressed business casual. But with his athletic build, he had the type of appealing, rugged good looks that had her wanting to trek through the great outdoors with him.

A close-fitting jacket, jeans and hiking boots. She could definitely see him out of his work clothes and wearing that ensemble. Wait. She shouldn't be picturing him in or out of his clothes. They had a business relationship, that was it.

Tess smirked. "You don't need to answer my question. The fact that you're almost drooling says everything."

Eliza dabbed the corner of her mouth with her napkin as warmth crept into her face. "If I am almost drooling, it's because of how good this roll is. And so what if he's cute?"

"Because the hotter they are, the more trouble they cause. This one client I had—I swear he thought his face was a form of currency."

Eliza released a breezy chuckle. "Oh, I know the type."

But Max wasn't aloof or full of himself. He had an ease and confidence about him that was genuine. And so was his laughter. Just before it rumbled out of his chest, amusement would bloom in his eyes.

"If he's unattached, the problem could be financial then. He might need to scale down his expectations to fit his bank account."

Actually, Max was financially solid. Or at least he should have been. The Maloney brothers had inherited money from a relative. A Fortune relative. If the rumors were true about the amount of the estate, it had a lot of zeroes at the end of it.

His brother Linc had received the money. Everyone was wondering which brother would be next to inherit their share.

Eliza held back on telling Tess the inside scoop.

Dishing up gossip wasn't her style. "He's an accountant, and he also does financial planning so I don't believe lack of money is the issue. Maybe he's not ready to buy a house. He's just in his early thirties. Home ownership is a huge investment. You know how that can freak some people out."

"You're being too generous. How old were you when you bought your first home here in San Antonio three years ago? Twenty-three?"

"Twenty-four. But because I worked in real estate, I understood the risks. And you were guiding me through the process all the way." With five more years of life experience under her stilettos than Eliza, Tess had taken her under her wing.

The vision of the back deck at her old home, shaded under a canopy of trees and surrounded by flowering bushes, came into Eliza's thoughts. That had been her favorite place in the house. It had been the perfect spot to enjoy coffee in the morning and entertain friends on a rare free weekend.

She and Tess had also spent plenty of hours there drinking glasses of wine. They'd commiserated over their busy schedules, and their latest swipe-right dates that hadn't worked out. And they'd also found reasons to laugh.

Three years ago, she'd sold the house and moved back to Chatelaine. Selling the home she'd loved and stretching her and Tess's sisterlike bond to a long-distance friendship had been hard. But her dad had been sick, and her parents had needed her. Family always came first.

"Whatever the reason is for him backing out, I know it's frustrating. Especially since there probably aren't a whole lot of properties to choose from in Chatelaine."

"Exactly."

"The two things we aren't worried about here in San Antonio are inventory and clients."

Eliza nibbled on her roll. Appreciation for the flavors of cinnamon and orange bursting in her mouth as well as envy over Tess's situation brought out a moan. "That sounds like real estate nirvana."

"You could be enjoying nirvana along with me." Tess gave Eliza a prolonged stare. "In case you missed it, that was a job offer."

Caught off guard, Eliza rearranged the napkin on her lap as she grappled with a response. "I'm flattered... and surprised."

"You shouldn't be. You're tenacious and a problem solver, which are qualities I want in my team members. And with your past experience working in San Antonio, I know you're more than capable of swimming in a bigger pond."

"I'm doing well in Chatelaine. I appreciate the offer, but—"

Tess briefly laid her hand on Eliza's. "Before you say no, hear me out. I have prospects waiting to buy property, and you have the skills to close the deals. Bottom line, there's money to be made. Why settle for just doing well when you could level up to really great? I'm finishing interviews for my team positions in three or four weeks. I don't need an answer until then. Will you just think about it?"

The sincerity in Tess's eyes stalled Eliza from turning her down. Agreeing to think about it wasn't a commitment. "All right. I will."

Eliza sipped her coffee. More money wasn't everything. She was content with her position and being close to family. Why would she leave Chatelaine?

Chapter Two

Max Fortune Maloney glanced at the photos of the house on his phone. Five bedrooms, a heated pool, an indoor basketball court. The only thing missing was a horse barn, but there was plenty of land to build one in the field adjacent to the backyard.

The construction plan that had come to mind when he'd viewed the place had included one or two stalls, but Eliza had suggested at least four. That way, space wouldn't become an issue should he decide to buy more horses.

But he wouldn't get the opportunity to build that horse barn, relax by the pool or perfect his jump shot on the court. The call he'd made to the real estate office that morning declining to make a bid on the property sealed the decision. Still, he didn't have a choice.

He and his brothers, Linc, Cooper, and Damon, along

with their sister, Justine, had recently found out they were inheriting money from their deceased long-lost grandfather, Wendell Fortune.

Martin Smith, the executor of Wendell's estate, had told them they would each receive their part of the inheritance at separate times. Martin had given Linc a check over a month ago during a family gathering held at their mother's house.

All Max had gotten from Martin so far, though, was delays.

He was so damn close to becoming a millionaire, but not close enough to purchase the house he wanted. How messed up was that?

"Hey." His friend and neighbor Greg called out to him from the other end of the deck attached to Greg's townhome. "Are we doing this or what?"

"Doing it."

"Then keep your eye on the ball and work faster." Greg lifted his ball cap and raked back his black hair. His gray eyes held hints of exasperation. "I want to get my new railing done and grill the steaks before the game comes on."

"You'll have time. Relax. This won't take long." Max tucked his phone into the back pocket of his jeans. As he pushed the sleeves of his gray sweatshirt up his forearms, he pointed to the new wood spindles and beams assembled on the back lawn for the deck railing. "The pieces are already cut. We just have to screw them together."

"This'll take forever if you don't stop looking at your phone every two seconds. Who is she?"

"She who?"

"The woman who's got your head all messed up."

At the sound of the new voice, Max turned to his dark-haired, younger brother Cooper strolling out of the open sliding door of Greg's place.

Dressed similarly to Max and Greg, he'd ditched his usual Stetson and cowboy boots for a faded blue ball cap and Timberland boots. "Linc thinks you're seeing someone new and she's local. Damon says you probably met someone when you were in Dallas a few weeks back."

Max huffed a breath. His brothers were speculating about his relationships. That wasn't new. If their sister, Justine, were around, instead living in Rambling Rose with her family, she would have been in on it, too. Knowing his brothers, there was money on the line. "And what's your theory?"

Coop shrugged. "It's obvious. You hooked up with an ex."

"I what?" Max choked out a laugh. "What makes you think that?"

"You've been antsy lately. Contact with your exes always makes you that way."

"No, it doesn't."

"It does." Greg stepped off the raised deck and walked to the wood on the grass. "When you and Ondine got back together, you constantly checked your phone."

"Same with Brenda," Coop added.

"And Whitley." Greg dropped spindles on the deck. "When you hooked back up with her, you couldn't tell east from west."

"You two are way off target. After we broke up, Ondine and I met a few times because she hired me to write a financial plan for her, and Brenda—we ran into each other when she came down from Dallas to visit her mom and we went to lunch, once. And me and Whitley..." The rest of Max's objection momentarily died on his lips. "That'll never happen again."

You're emotionally unavailable.

That's what Whitley had told him six months ago before she'd moved to San Diego.

They'd been in an on-again, off-again situation for over a year. During their last "on-again" phase, she kept hinting about them entering into a more serious relationship. One that included the possibility of marriage. He couldn't lie to her. That type of commitment wasn't on his radar—now or anytime in the future.

"How much is the bet?" Max asked.

"Twenty bucks each from the losers, and a paid beer tab for a month. So who won?" From Coop's self-assured grin, he was already counting the money.

"None of you."

"What?" Coop shook his head. "No way. I know I'm right."

"No, you lost. I'm not involved with anyone."

"For now." Greg chuckled. "The bachelor auction might change that."

Max snorted a laugh. "Yeah, that's definitely not happening. One date and I'm done."

The last thing he wanted was to be tied down in a relationship. And if it were up to him, he wouldn't be in the Valentine's Day Bachelor Auction at all. Someone had pulled him into the event sponsored by the Chatelaine Fish and Wildlife Conservation Society. Coop and Damon were in it, too.

Linc was the lucky one. He got out of it because of his hot and heavy relationship with Remi Reynolds.

Since the breakup with Whitley, Max had decided to give the dating scene a rest, but the auction was for charity. He couldn't say no.

On the plus side, ever since the participants had been announced, more women had been smiling at him. That he could handle. In fact, he liked it. But the past few times he'd stopped by the Saddle & Spur Roadhouse to pick up a food order, he'd run into a blonde he recognized from around town. She'd had on a staff shirt from the GreatStore, the largest superstore in the area. According to her badge, her name was Alana.

The way she'd stared at him was like she was sizing up a special on the menu—and not in a good way. She'd made him nervous. And worse, the vibe she was giving off had reminded him of Whitley when she'd suddenly gotten more clingy during the last phase of their relationship.

Greg put more pieces of wood on the deck. He had army reserve duty the week of the auction, so his lucky ass wasn't a part of it. "Well, something's got you caught up. What's going on?"

"House hunting. It's not easy finding the right place."

"The right place?" Greg's good-natured laugh boomed out. "That's changed every week. What happened to the one with the basketball court?"

Max stepped down to the grass. He shouldn't have told Greg or anyone else about the homes he'd almost bid on. But he'd been so sure the house would be his. "I changed my mind."

Greg clapped Max on the back. "Like I told you before, not finding the house you want is a sign that you should buy the town house you're renting and just hang out for a few weeks on the beach."

Max laughed. "Yeah, you just want a free vacation."

"Damn right. I need to tag along to keep you out of trouble." Grinning, Greg headed toward the side of the town house. "I'll be right back. I left the screws we need in the garage."

Maybe Greg was right. But the part of Max that wanted to walk out of his front door and see nothing but wide-open spaces and trees instead of a row of duplexes immediately squashed doubt.

Coop nudged him. "So what really happened with the house? The last time I saw you, you said it was practically a done deal."

Max picked up a few beams and brought them to the deck. Evading the question would be easier, but if anyone could understand his situation, Coop could.

"It would have been a done deal if the money had shown up. But I haven't received my part of Wendell's estate yet."

"What?" Coop started lining up the spindles in between two of the beams. "Shouldn't you have gotten the money by now? What did Martin say?"

"Last we talked, he said there was an issue with the bank transfer. That was on Friday. I'm not sure what's going on now. I've left messages on his voice mail, but he hasn't returned my calls."

"Have you reached out to Linc? He might know another way to contact him. Or maybe he could lend you the money for the house. He knows you're good for it."

"I'm not bothering Linc about this. He should be enjoying his share of the inheritance, not worrying about mine."

Max was also advising Linc about investing his money. From a professional point of view, asking for a loan from someone he was advising, family or not, wouldn't be a smart move.

Coop dug out a tape measure and pencil from a blue toolbox near the wall. "I'm sorry things didn't work out. I know you really liked that house. Losing it has to suck."

"It does." Max brought over the last of the beams, then stepped back up on the deck. "But messing up with Eliza is bothering me, too."

"I thought you said a woman wasn't in the picture?"

"Eliza and I are not involved like that." Max took the tape measure from Coop's outstretched hand. He pulled the yellow-and-black metal tape partway out, and Coop took the end of it. "She's my real estate agent. I know she's frustrated with me about not making an offer on the house, and she has every right to be. This is the third time I've flaked out on an offer."

Coop hunkered down with Max, and they lined up the tape measure with one of the beams. "Did you tell her about the money not coming in as expected?"

"No." Max locked down the tape, and Coop moved

toward him making hash marks with the pencil on the wood every four inches. "Like everyone else in town, she's heard about the inheritance. How will it sound if I'm giving her some financial excuse? She'll think I'm just wasting her time."

"You're right. That wouldn't be good." Coop made the last hash mark on the beam and they both stood. "Heck, she might even drop you as a client."

"Thanks for the support."

"Just calling things like I see it." Coop tucked the pencil behind his ear and grinned. "Everyone knows your track record with women ain't the best."

"It's better than yours." Max thumped his brother's arm, and Coop easily absorbed the hit.

With Coop's daredevil tendencies, he was too busy leaping in and out of trouble to focus on his relationships. They usually didn't last long.

Coop's smile sobered a little. "But seriously. Maybe you should just be honest with her. Not admitting what's going on is just making you look shady."

"I hope she doesn't see it that way."

Eliza dropping him as a client... She wouldn't... would she? He didn't want another agent. She understood him. And despite the difficulties in finding what he'd asked for in a home, she'd never tried to sway him from his vision.

Greg returned and they got back to work.

By the late afternoon, the new railing was installed. Done eating their steaks, they were kicking back on the gray L-shaped couch in Greg's living room.

As cheers from the basketball game reverberated

from a flat-screen TV that took up most of the wall, Max's phone buzzed on the coffee table with an incoming call. Leaning forward, he glanced at the screen.

Recognizing the number, he quickly answered it. "Hello."

"Hi, Max. It's Eliza. Do you have a minute to talk?"

The seriousness in her voice made him sit straighter in the seat. She usually sounded upbeat. "Yes. I'm glad you called." Noticing Greg's and Coop's inquisitive expressions, he got up and went into the kitchen.

"I thought I should reach out to you about our search for your new home. The last three properties—you changed your mind about moving forward."

"Yeah, about that... I'm sorry."

"The important thing is you didn't buy the wrong house. Finding the right place can take time. That's why you shouldn't feel pressured to make an offer on one unless you're absolutely sure. It's also okay if you've changed your mind and you're not quite ready to look for a home."

"I'm more than ready. And I was sure...especially with the last house you showed me."

As Max rubbed the back of his neck, he glanced out the side window at the finished railing. What Coop said to him earlier about looking shady by not being honest with Eliza came to mind. The last thing he wanted was for her to see him as untrustworthy or unreliable. His father, Rick, and his grandfather Wendell had been experts in that department.

Despite all the money Wendell made in silver mining when he was alive, the man had chosen to abandon his family, including his son Rick.

Rick had never known his father, and was presumably never even aware of his Fortune roots. Still, he'd pretty much followed in Wendell's footsteps when it came to his family. He'd walked out and never looked back.

No matter what it took, Max planned on steering clear of those family traits.

And more importantly, Eliza had been up front with him about the challenges in searching for his home. He needed to be just as open with her about his financial situation.

"The truth is I've been expecting some money. An inheritance from my grandfather. But there's been a slight delay with it landing in my bank account."

"Oh… I see. Should we put a hold on everything, then?"

"No. The money is coming. Soon. I'd rather keep looking. If it's okay with you."

Apprehension knotted in his gut during the silence. Was she trying to decide how to tell him she was cutting him loose?

"All right. We can keep looking." Relief ran through him. "But, Max—from this point on, let's hold off on making any offers until the money's actually in the bank."

"Not a problem. I can live with that."

"Good. A few homes on the south side of town just came up for sale. Can you meet up with me on Tuesday?"

"I sure can."

"Okay. I'll let Sharon know, and she'll contact you with the details."

They said their goodbyes.

Max switched to the message app on his phone and sent a text.

Martin, I really need you to call me.

Chapter Three

"What do you think?" Eliza lifted her arms from her sides as she glanced around the expansive family room.

Max stuck his hands in the pockets of his short, dark overcoat, considering what to say. "It's nice. Lots of space."

"The size of this place is impressive."

It was—from the floor-to-ceiling brick fireplace in the living room to the square footage of the bedrooms to the swimming pool just outside the bay window. But it didn't have an indoor, air-conditioned basketball court.

"And look at this view." Eliza walked to the window in the empty room.

Dressed in a tailored gray pantsuit and high-heeled black pumps, she fit with the space. Maybe he did, too. He just needed to envision himself there.

Max conjured up an image of sitting in the room on

the new leather sectional he was going to splurge on once
he got a new place. He wouldn't have on the long-sleeved
burgundy sweater and navy pants he wore now—a
T-shirt and jeans were more like it.

A bottle of beer and a sausage pizza laid out on a
coffee table. He could see that, too, along with a movie
playing on a flat-screen television mounted on the far
wall.

Imagining it that way definitely helped, but it still
wasn't complete. Maybe adding another person would
make a difference.

Surprisingly, Eliza materialized next to him in the
vision. He went with it. She was there now, standing in
the room with him. It made sense that she would pop
into his mind. And this was about trying to visualize
being in the space with someone. Not necessarily Eliza.
Still, he wondered. What was she like outside work?
Was she the type who liked to watch a new movie or
did she prefer to binge-watch an entire television series? Did she like beer and pizza? Or was she a wine
and canapé girl?

The thought of discovering what she did like piqued
his interest. Once he found a place and moved in, maybe
he could invite her over or he could take her out. It
wouldn't be a date, but a thank you for putting up with
him as a client.

Eliza walked over to him, and the daydream dissipated in the fragrance of her perfume—soft, floral and
wholly feminine.

Today her hair was in a messy bun. But just like when

she wore it down, tendrils hung near her cheeks. In a minute, she would smooth them behind her ears.

Just as he predicted, she tucked the strands away, and the silver, interlocking loops hanging from her delicate earlobes winked in the light.

She always wore pretty earrings. But those must have been new. He'd never noticed her wearing them before.

Eliza's chestnut-colored eyes met his, and her brow furrowed. "You don't see yourself here, do you?"

Did he? Maybe under the right conditions... But the experience of enjoying beer and pizza with her didn't come with the house. "No. I don't."

"That's okay." Her reassuring smile brought a faint dimple to her cheek. "The place for you is out there. We'll find it."

"Is it possible to find the right house twice?"

She shrugged. "It is if you're willing to expand into other possibilities. I know you really liked the house with the basketball court, but if you keep comparing every home you see to that one, you'll never move past it."

Was he that transparent about missing the basketball court or was she just that intuitive? "I'll keep that in mind."

They walked out the front door.

Max zipped up his coat and flipped up the collar as protection from the slight chill in the air.

Eliza closed up the house and put the key back in the lockbox. "I'm sorry none of the homes we looked at today worked out. One of my contacts mentioned there might be some places opening up on the west side of town. I'll check into it and get back to you before the end of the week."

They were done? But it was only ten o'clock. He'd cleared his calendar through his part-time receptionist, Jill, until early afternoon.

"Sharon had mentioned something about an open house?" Max asked. "When's that happening?"

Eliza shivered. "It's today. But the house is older than what you wanted."

"You said I should expand into other possibilities."

"It's also farther out."

And he'd mentioned he wasn't interested in a long commute from his office just outside town. But he'd blocked off the morning and most of the afternoon in anticipation of being with her. And he wasn't in a hurry to return to his office.

She shivered again, and Max reached for the zipper of his coat planning to shrug it off and give it to her. But he was her client, not a friend, and she'd probably refuse to take it.

But he could hurry things along to get her out of the cold and into her warm car. "If you have time, I'd still like to see it."

"Okay, let's go." Smiling, Eliza hurried toward her red sedan. "But don't say I didn't warn you."

A short time later, he followed her out of the driveway.

She zoomed ahead of him on the two-way road, and as he eased down on the accelerator, the navy truck's engine softly rumbled.

His phone rang in the holder on the dashboard, and a name scrolled across the screen. *It's about time...*

Max used the crew cab's interface system to answer. "Hello, Martin."

"Hey there, Max." Martin's voice came through the speakers. "Sorry about not getting back to you right away. But I have good news. I've hunted down the reason why you didn't get your money. There was a paperwork glitch. But it's an easy fix."

"That *is* good news. When should I expect the deposit?"

"Soon. They just have to send me some new papers for you to sign."

"When will I receive them?"

"I was hoping we could meet tomorrow. They need my signature, too. We can sign them together, and then I can send them off right away."

"Give me a time and a place and I'll be there."

"How 'bout I call you when I get to Chatelaine, and we can decide all of that then?"

Or they could just agree on a time and place now. He could ask, but knowing Martin, he wouldn't commit. *More waiting.* But the man had finally returned his call and delivered fairly good news about receiving the money. That was progress.

Max tamped down exasperation. "Sure." He glanced at Eliza's car ahead of him. "But if we could move things along, I would really appreciate it. Remember, I told you I wanted to buy a house?"

"I do. Did you find one?"

"I did, but because I didn't have the money, I couldn't follow through on the bid I promised to make. My real estate agent wasn't happy about it. She's been working hard to find the right house for me. It hasn't been easy. And that wasn't the first time I backed out on making an offer."

"Ahh, I understand. Disappointing a pretty woman isn't a good position to be in."

His concern was about missing out on the house. Max opened his mouth to correct him but paused. Martin may have misinterpreted the issue, but he wasn't wrong about Eliza. She was a very pretty woman, and he didn't like her being disappointed in him.

"But don't worry," Martin added. "We'll fix the situation."

"I'm looking forward to it."

They said their goodbyes and Max hung up. *We'll* fix the situation? It wasn't like he had a choice in what was happening. Martin controlled everything.

Twenty minutes later, he parked his truck next to Eliza's car in the wide, extended driveway of a two-story, Spanish-style home. He got out of his car and stood there, his gaze fixed on the light-colored stucco house.

Large arched windows on both floors were framed in deep rust-colored brick that matched the clay tiles on the multipitched roof. On the top floor to the left, French doors opened onto a balcony with a wrought iron railing.

A vision rose in his mind of standing there with a cup of coffee watching the first rays of a yellow-and-orange-hued sunrise. Goose bumps rose on his arms.

"Max?" Eliza waited up ahead. She'd put on a black fitted coat. "Have you changed your mind about seeing the house?"

"No. I'm coming." He joined her and they walked up the brick path to the front door.

The front lawn was neatly clipped. And so were the shrubs interspersed with terra-cotta pots holding a variety of plants in front of the house.

The pride the owners took in the place made him curious about the inside. Especially the room where the balcony was located.

"Why are the owners selling?"

"I'm not sure. I heard they're an older couple. They could be downsizing." Eliza glanced around. "That's strange. I expected a lot more people to be here. And I only saw one sign on the road advertising the open house."

"Do you think it's over already?" He hoped not.

"Anything's possible, but the notice I received said it was happening until three. The lack of advertising could be more about the owners. They're selling the place themselves, and maybe they chose not to put up a lot of signs." Eliza rang the bell.

A few moments later, an older woman with short, salt-and-pepper hair and wearing jeans, a plaid green shirt and sneakers opened the door. "Hello."

"Hello." Eliza smiled. "We're here for the open house. Is it still happening?"

An apologetic expression fell over the woman's face. "We had to end things early. My husband isn't feeling well. I'm so sorry for the inconvenience."

"No apology necessary," Eliza said.

"We're sorry to have disturbed you," Max added. "I hope he feels better soon."

"Nancy, who's at the door? Did the Jessups come back?" a man called from inside.

"No. It's another couple. They came by to look at the house."

A man with neatly clipped gray hair and wearing wire-rimmed glasses walked up beside the woman. Like her, he was dressed casually in a button-down shirt and jeans, but he had on slippers.

The woman laid her hand on his arm. "Cal, you're supposed to be resting."

"I'm fine." A hint of a Texas drawl wove through Cal's words. He looked at Max and Eliza. "You're too late. We're done showing the house."

A gust of wind swirled through the doorway, and flyers sitting on a table in the entryway flew outside.

"Oh no." Nancy hurried out the door trying to snatch them before they scattered over the yard.

Max and Eliza snagged the papers with information about the house that were still on the porch.

Cal stooped down near the doorway and picked one up. As he stood straight, he winced as if in pain.

"Cal," Nancy called out. "You shouldn't be out here. It's too cold. Go back inside."

Ignoring her, Cal reached for another flyer. "I can help."

Nancy looked torn between keeping an eye on Cal and chasing down the flyers. "I can do it. Why don't you show this nice couple the house? They came all the way out here to see it."

"If you wouldn't mind, we'd love to take a look." Eliza met Max's gaze, but her voice was loud enough for the couple to hear. "I'll stay and help gather the flyers. You can tour the house. While I'm out here, I can find out about the landscaping. I'm interested in a similar design."

Max connected with the compassion in Eliza's eyes. They were on the same page about helping Nancy get Cal back inside. "That's a good idea. Let's do that."

He walked to Cal and extended his hand. "Hello, sir. I'm Max Fortune Maloney. If you could spare the time, I would appreciate a tour of the house."

The older man shook his hand. "Cal Pickett." He peered over his glasses. "I guess a brief look around won't hurt. But my wife needs her coat."

"I can take it to her." Max accepted the green jacket Cal handed him from the hook by the door and went to Nancy. He held it open for her while she slipped it on.

"Let's get after it, young man," Cal yelled. "I don't have all day."

Nancy met Max's gaze. "His bark really is worse than his bite."

"We'll be fine." Max smiled at her.

Eliza looked a tad concerned, and he gave her a wink before jogging back to the older man. As a financial adviser, he'd dealt with demanding clients. He could handle Cal.

Inside the house, Cal shut the door behind them. "Like the papers that flew out the door said, we built the house in eighty-five. It sits on five acres of land. We wanted plenty of room for our family. The main area is this way."

Following Cal's impatient directing gestures, Max walked to the living room.

High ceilings, multiple windows, and a large sliding

door leading to a back deck provided lots of natural light. The decor boasting dark leather and stained wood furniture complemented the outside landscape.

But the smell wafting in the air was just as appealing as the view.

A taste memory ignited, and Max's mouth watered. "You're cooking beef stew." That had been one of his mom's go-to meals when he was a kid.

"Yes. My wife just finished making it when you rang the doorbell."

Max followed Cal's gaze. Across a large black granite-topped island separating the living room from the kitchen, a pot with steam rising from it sat on the stainless-steel stove.

Growing up, he, his brothers and his sister had crowded around the kitchen counter for meals. The granite island was an updated version of that but with a lot more room.

Cal rested his hands heavily on the island. "We remodeled the kitchen a year ago. All the cabinets and appliances are new. The formal dining room is through that archway over there by the breakfast nook. We don't go in there much anymore except when the grandkids are here. But they mostly like to sit out on the deck or in the sunroom."

Cal pointed to the nook with a kitchen table and chairs and a picture window. Outside was a deck, and beyond that, what looked to be a huge backyard.

Most likely, the adults in the family watched the grandkids from there just like his mom used to keep an eye on him and his siblings from her spot at the window over the kitchen sink.

As a single mom, with four rambunctious boys and one daughter, Kimberly Maloney had kept a close watch on them all the time, including while she washed dishes. Sometimes it seemed like she had the ability to read their minds before they'd even thought about getting into trouble.

"There's a spare bedroom down the rear hall." Cal pointed away from the kitchen. "My wife has already packed things up in the rooms on the second floor so we sleep there now instead of upstairs in the primary bedroom. Nothing much to see. It has a bathroom attached that we remodeled at the same time as the kitchen. Same view of the backyard that you see in here."

The older man shuffled toward the front of the house.

Max had questions about what else was down the rear hall, but he held on to them. It was obvious Cal wanted to move things along. Maybe the older man did want to rest. And Max liked everything so far. Chances were, he'd like that part of the house, too.

Cal stopped at the bottom of the stairs and pointed to the second floor. "It'll be faster if you go up on your own. The primary bedroom is to the left at the end of the hall. The rest of the rooms are to the right."

"Thank you." Max walked up the stairs to an expansive landing with a banister. The area overlooked the living room.

He went down the hall to the left first. The spacious bedroom with a spa-style bathroom did not disappoint. And neither did the attached balcony.

As he took in the view of the yard, and beyond that, the field bordered by trees, a sense of peace and excitement settled over him. Unlike the house he and Eliza just left, he could see himself here. It didn't have the things on his list for a home, but for some odd reason, it felt like a perfect fit.

Below, Eliza and Cal's wife were having an animated conversation as they pointed to flowering plants near the hedges.

They really were talking about the landscaping.

Looking up, Eliza spotted him, and he gave her a brief wave.

After checking out the rest of the rooms that had packed moving boxes stacked along the walls, he headed back down to the first floor. Just like downstairs, the upstairs was in great shape. Yes, it was a longer drive to his office, and there wasn't a swimming pool, basketball court or a horse barn. But there was lots of space, an unbeatable view and plenty of land to build what he wanted.

As he walked downstairs, Cal looked up at him. "Are you done seeing everything?"

"I am. You have a great home."

"If Nancy and I didn't have to move, we wouldn't. But my wife wants to be closer to our children and the grandkids. The one thing she and I both agree on is that we're selling this place to a family. You don't seem to fit the bill."

"No, I don't have any immediate plans for children. Maybe that will change. Someday."

"Someday?" Cal crossed his arms over his chest. "What does *she* say about that?"

It took a second for Max to connect the dots. "You mean Eliza? I'm not sure how she feels about kids. We're—"

"Poor communication. That's why couples today don't stay together. Nancy and I wouldn't have lasted for over fifty years without talking about the important things. I know what you're thinking, son."

Max doubted Cal did know, but his mom taught him to respect his elders. And the man was pretty worked up over the family issue. It was best to let Cal finish before he corrected him.

The front door opened, and Eliza and Nancy walked in.

"Whew, that was work. But I think we got them all." Nancy pointed to the stack of flyers Eliza was carrying. "I'll take those. Thanks again for your help."

"You're welcome." Eliza handed her the papers. "And thanks for telling me about your house."

"My pleasure." As Nancy hung up her coat, she sniffed the air. "Excuse me. I better check on lunch before it burns."

As she hurried off, Eliza turned to Max. "Did you hear about the horse barn out back? Nancy said it needs to be rebuilt but the foundation is solid."

"No, we didn't get to that yet."

Max recalled the structure he'd spotted in the distance from the rear bedroom window. That must have been the barn. But he didn't need to see it. He already knew what he wanted to do. He'd planned on addressing the couple together, but Cal seemed ready for them to leave, and he didn't want to keep them from enjoying lunch.

"Sir, I want to make an offer on your home. I'll meet your asking price. No negotiation."

Eliza gasped. "What?"

Cal looked him in the eye. "No."

Chapter Four

No? Cal's response caught Max by surprise.

Just as he was about to sweeten the offer by 10 percent, Cal cut him off with a raised hand. "Save your breath. Nancy and I agreed that we're only selling this house to a family, and we've found one. The Jessups. They have five-year-old twin boys and a baby on the way. They're the perfect match, and no amount of money will change our minds." He opened the door and waved Max and Eliza out. "Best of luck finding a place. Goodbye."

As soon as they were both outside, Cal shut the door behind them.

"Wow," Eliza muttered. "I don't know who I'm shocked at the most. You or him."

"Me?" Max went after her as she walked down the pathway. "I wasn't the one being rude."

"We had an agreement. No making offers on another

house until your money was in the bank." The tap of her heels grew heavier as she moved farther ahead of him.

He caught up with her near the driveway. "I hadn't planned on making an offer. But you said the right home could come along again, and it has. This one." If only Cal would sell it to him.

The rigidness in Eliza's shoulders diminished with a long exhale. She faced him. "Max, you can't keep doing this. I think you should step back from house hunting until you receive the money you've been waiting for."

"It's coming."

She opened her mouth to speak but paused. Frowning, she stared past his shoulder.

He followed her gaze.

Nancy trotted from a door on the side of the house. When she reached them, she was out of breath. "I'm so glad I caught you. I don't have much time. Cal thinks I'm giving you my plant food recipe for the shrubs." She looked to Max. "Cal said you want to buy the house?"

"I do. But he said you'd already found a buyer."

"The Jessups—but I overheard them talking. The wife loves the house and wants to buy it, but the husband said no. Our asking price is way out of their budget. I honestly don't think we'll hear back from them. You've made us a generous offer, and we need to take it."

"But what about only selling to a family?" Eliza asked. "Your husband sounded adamant about it."

"What he really wants is for one of our kids to take over the house, but our son and daughter are happy in Fort Worth. Selling to a family is the second-best option.

I used to see it that way, too, but we can't afford to be sentimental anymore." Sadness came into Nancy's eyes. "Cal has rheumatoid arthritis. Last week, we found out that it's in his lungs and spine now. The best thing for us to do is move to Fort Worth. Being near our children will simplify our lives and put us closer to the medical care he needs."

Max recalled Cal's mobility issues. The older man was clearly in pain. "I'm sorry to hear he's not well."

"So am I." Empathy filled Eliza's tone. "But even if Max made a formal offer on the house, we can't move forward without Cal's approval."

"I'll change his mind," Nancy looked between Eliza and Max. "Please, give me a day or two. I know I can convince him, especially since he believes you're together."

"What?" Eliza's tone rose slightly. "Together like as a couple? No. I'm just Max's real estate agent."

"For some reason Cal got the impression you two are in a serious relationship."

Poor communication. That's why couples today don't stay together...

As Max recalled the older man's comment, Nancy and Eliza stared at him. "No. I never told Cal we were a couple. He assumed we were, and I didn't get a chance to correct him."

"I'm glad you didn't," Nancy said. "If I emphasize that you're just starting out, like we were once upon a time, he'll soften to the idea of selling to you. Especially since having a family will be in your future."

"But it's not in our future." Eliza looked to Max as if seeking his support. "We're not even dating. I'm just helping him find a house."

"But maybe you could pretend to be together? I know it sounds like a wild idea, and I don't want to lie to Cal. But it takes two of us to look after this place, and with his health the way it is…he just can't do his part anymore."

Max filled in what Nancy wasn't saying. Taking care of Cal and the house fell on her shoulders. She was carrying the burden of handling everything on her own, like his mom had after his father, Rick, had run out on them. Nancy was in a stressful situation, and she was probably reaching the limit of what she could take. Otherwise, she wouldn't have asked him and Eliza to pretend to be together.

He had the financial resources—or he would have them in a few days. How could he not assist Nancy?

"Talk to Cal," Max said. "See what he says, and in the meantime, we'll discuss our options." He met Eliza's gaze, willing her to give him a chance to state his case.

She didn't look happy about it, but she nodded. "We'll discuss it."

"Thank you." Nancy shook both their hands. "I better get back to Cal. I have Eliza's business card. I'll call you when I get an answer." She hurried back inside.

Max stuck his hands in the pockets of his coat. Hopefully, Nancy's conversation with Cal would go well.

In the meantime, he had some convincing of his own to do.

* * *

Reining in frustration, Eliza stuck her hands in her pockets and faced Max, mirroring his stance. "What Nancy is asking us to do...we can't."

"I know it seems that way, but there's another side to it." He pressed a button on his key fob and his vehicle roared to life. "Can we talk about it in the truck where it's warmer? Please?"

The earnestness in his eyes and the breeze whipping around them prompted her to get into the front passenger seat. But there wasn't much to say.

Max joined her inside and shut the door.

The heat blowing through the vents stirred up the alluring smells of buttery leather mixed with a hint of his woodsy cologne.

He adjusted the temperature control. "Is that okay or do you want me to turn it up?"

"It's fine." The comfortable interior tempted her to sit back and enjoy it, but she wasn't there to get cozy. "I feel for Nancy and Cal, just like you do, but lying to him is wrong."

"Nancy isn't asking us to lie. She just wants us to go along with what he already believes. And for a good reason."

"And what reason is that?" Anticipating immediate pushback from the position of him wanting the house, she geared up for an argument. His pause caught her off guard.

Resting a hand on the bottom of the steering wheel, Max sighed and sat back in the seat. "Do I want the house? Yes. But I want to help Cal and Nancy, too. She doesn't want to deceive Cal for selfish reasons. He's sick, and she's trying to take care of him. Me buying the house would lessen some of the load."

That was a valid point but… "What about the delay with your inheritance? You can't buy the house if you don't have the money."

"The executor of my grandfather's estate called me on the way here. I'm about to receive it. He and I just need to sign some papers."

"When are you doing that?"

"I'm thinking sometime tomorrow."

Eliza caught a glimpse of uncertainty on his face. "I know you want to help the Picketts. But you can't promise them what you don't have."

"But I *will* have the money. I know this probably sounds strange because of what I said about the last house I wanted, but this one is for me. I can't explain why, but I feel it."

"Max, I do understand."

"If you understand, then you know how much buying this place means to me. I don't have my inheritance yet, but I do have money in the bank. And I have this truck. I just bought it outright. I'll sell it *and* empty my accounts to give the Picketts a down payment if I have to. I'll even get a letter of credit from the estate to prove I'm good for the rest."

Eliza was drawn to what she saw in his eyes. Certainty. It hadn't been there with the other house. Back then, he'd discovered a nice property with something that intrigued him—a basketball court. Today, he'd clearly found a place he wanted to call home.

Max turned more toward Eliza. Sincerity and determination joined the certainty in his gaze. "I can give Nancy and Cal a way out of their situation. But I need your help."

The next afternoon, Eliza sat at her desk in her office. Sharon, and Regina "Reggie" Vale, the owner of the Vale Real Estate group, were both out of the building.

The business was in a corner house that had been converted into a modern work space and was located at the end of a street in a well-tended neighborhood outside of the main area of Chatelaine.

What would have been the entryway and living room had been turned into reception area with dark wood furniture and decorated in hues of aqua, yellow and orange like the rest of the office. Maps detailing Chatelaine and the surrounding area were in wood frames on the walls.

Sharon's desk sat near the middle of the space in front of the door to the meeting room on one side, a kitchenette where visitors could grab coffee and or a cold drink from a beverage station on the other, and the middle hallway that led to Eliza's and Reggie's offices

Unable to concentrate on her computer screen, Eliza looked out the window past the bushes and small parking lot to the street beyond.

Except for the occasional car driving by it was fairly quiet. If only her mind was less chaotic.

She'd awakened earlier than usual that morning. Her conversation with Max in the truck yesterday kept playing through her mind, along with the memory of Nancy's hopeful expression.

I can give Nancy and Cal a way out of their situation. But I need your help.

How far he was willing to go to assist the couple was generous and impressive. His genuineness along with his reasoning had swayed her into taking more time to consider what Nancy was asking them to do.

Pretending to be a couple. She hadn't done anything like that since... When? Her senior year in college?

Back then, one of her study partners had asked her to attend a wedding as his girlfriend.

He'd been friends with the bride and groom, but a year prior, he'd been engaged to the bride. Even though he'd been on good terms with the couple, he'd wanted to show up to the wedding with a girlfriend to dispel any rumors about him having hard feelings about the marriage.

She'd filled in for the role, and they'd had a great time pretending. They'd even kissed.

It hadn't been unpleasant. But the kiss hadn't inspired excitement or curiosity over what might happen between them once they left the reception. Knowing they were destined for separate hotel rooms at the end of the night had made it easier for them to have fun together. The lines were clear. They were strictly in the friend zone.

But that had been a fun, simple outing. Nancy was asking her and Max to pretend, from now until the closing of the house, that they were in a serious relationship and even thinking about starting a family. That was much more intense.

Yes, she enjoyed being around Max as they looked

for his perfect home. And if they had met under different circumstances, she might have gone out with him if he'd asked. But they were strangers. What if they had to lay on some PDA in front of Cal? Serious couples stood close to each other, they hugged, held hands.

They kissed.

Not that kissing Max would be a hardship. He had nice, firm-looking lips, and he didn't seem like he was that guy who'd failed to get the kissing memo in college—use lip balm and don't stick your tongue down a woman's throat.

And from her experience, guys like Max, who were equally comfortable taking the lead and stepping aside when they didn't have to take charge, usually knew how to deliver a kiss. Not too hard or soft, but with *just* the right amount of contact.

A daydream rose in her mind of Max standing in front of her with a small sexy smile on his lips. He hesitated for just a beat, gauging her readiness before leaning in.

Oh yes… If Max looked at her like that, she would definitely be ready.

The sound of the front door opening yanked Eliza from her fantasy, and she glanced at the security monitor near the computer on her desk.

On-screen, Reggie walked through the reception area.

Her footsteps echoed down the hallway as she approached, and a short time later, the youthful-looking woman in her mid to late sixties popped her head into the office.

The white pullover sweater and chunky silver necklace she'd paired with navy slacks and pumps perfectly complemented her wavy white hair.

"Welcome back." Reggie smiled. "How was the conference?" She'd been out of the office for the past two days, and this was her first time seeing Eliza that week.

"Thank you. It was great. I did enjoy it for the most part. But it was also a long few days."

"I can imagine. Conferences take a lot out of you. Whenever I return from one, I need a break. I hope you got some rest on Sunday."

Eliza sat back in the burgundy desk chair. "For the most part I did." After brunch with Tess, she'd gone straight home to the cottage she lived in on her parents' property. "I tackled some laundry, had dinner and watched a movie with my dad. After that, I went to bed early."

"Throw in a little housecleaning and you've almost described my entire weekend." Chuckling, Reggie turned to leave but stopped. "Oh—I almost forgot. Did you go by Cal and Nancy Pickett's open house? I was sorry I missed it, but I haven't heard anything about it coming under contract yet. I might have a client who's interested in seeing it."

"Does your client have a family? If they don't, that might not be the property to show them."

"Why not?"

"Cal only wants to sell the house to a family. And he was pretty adamant about it."

Reggie huffed a chuckle. "I'm not surprised by that. Cal always was particular about things. But Nancy, she's always been levelheaded. I'm surprised she's agreeing with him."

"Do you know them well?"

"I'm acquainted with them." Reggie walked into the office and sat in one of the two chairs in front of the desk. "Cal worked as a livestock inspector before he retired. Quite a few local people had dealings with him, including my parents. I know Nancy a bit better. We were in 4-H together. But I haven't seen or spoken to them in a long time. They're a little reclusive, and they don't come to town very often."

"Then you might not have heard. Cal has rheumatoid arthritis, and he's experiencing some major health challenges. The open house ended early because he wasn't feeling well."

"Oh no." Concern came into Reggie's face. "I hadn't heard he was sick. Is that why they're selling?"

"Yes. They're moving closer to their children."

"Well if that's the case, I'm surprised they're restricting buyers to just families."

"It's more Cal's than Nancy's doing. My client, Max Fortune Maloney, offered Cal the full asking price, but he turned it down."

"What a difficult situation for Nancy to be in. I hope she can convince Cal to see reason."

"She thinks she can, but…" Eliza paused, not sure how to explain things. But Reggie wasn't just her boss. She was also one of her mentors and had always given her good advice. "Nancy asked Max and me to pretend we're in a relationship and thinking about having a family. Somehow, Cal got the wrong impression about us, and he already thinks we're a couple."

"Really?"

"I know." Eliza waited for Reggie to chime in with shock over Nancy's request.

Reggie's expression grew pensive. "How does Max feel about it?"

"Max? Well…he's willing to go along with it. But it's a terrible plan."

"Is it?"

Eliza met Reggie's gaze and was surprised at what she saw in her eyes. "You think I should say yes?"

"You have to make up your own mind about it. But can I share something with you, not as your boss but as someone who's been in a similar situation to Nancy's?"

"Of course. I always appreciate your point of view."

Reggie settled back in the chair. "Ten years ago, my mother was still alive. She lived on her own in the next town, and despite struggling with the upkeep of the house and her health, she refused to move. Whenever I brought it up, she told me to focus on my life and stop meddling in hers."

"But you changed her mind."

"Actually, I didn't. Mother Nature did. A tornado tore off part of the roof on the house. My mom thought she'd let the insurance policy lapse, but she'd forgotten I was handling the payments. I never told her differently. She moved here with me. At first, she wasn't happy about it, but within a few weeks, she reconnected with old friends and made new ones. She even got closer to me and the kids, and she was really there for me during my divorce. During those six years of living here, she was the happiest I'd seen her in a long time."

Reggie's words and the contentment in her nostalgic smile resonated. "Being closer to family can make a real difference."

Two and half years ago, Eliza's father, Benjamin Henry, had experienced complications after his heart attack, and frustration over his slow recovery had hit him hard. She, her mom, Iris, and members of their extended family had rallied around him, and his optimism slowly returned. She'd moved home to support her mom and continue to help with his recuperation.

Her dad was fully recovered now, enjoying life as a semiretired farrier.

Last year, her mom had gone back to work full-time as a logistics coordinator for an international aid group. She worked from home in Chatelaine but also visited the organization's offices as needed in California. Currently, she was away on business and had been gone a week.

Reggie stood. "I have to meet a client. When it comes to Cal and Nancy, just remember, there is no right or wrong decision. I understand why you wouldn't want to get involved. I'm with you either way."

"Thanks, Reggie. I appreciate the story about your mom and the advice."

Her boss left and Eliza returned to her thoughts.

No, she wasn't obligated to get involved with the situation. But going along with what Nancy asked would give Nancy, Cal and Max what they needed and wanted.

And as far as pretending, since the Picketts didn't

come into town, it wasn't like she and Max would have to make an announcement or put on a big show for everyone in Chatelaine. Conceivably, they would only have to pretend they were a couple around Cal, and if they planned it out right, that wouldn't be very often.

As if on cue, Eliza's phone chimed on her desk and Max's number lit up on-screen. She answered. "Hello, Max."

"Hi. I just heard from Martin Smith, the executor of my grandfather's estate. We're signing the papers this evening."

"That's good news. You're one step closer to getting what you want."

"It is good news, but as far as moving closer to what I want, I know us pretending to be a couple is a big ask. I'm okay with your decision either way. I want you to do what feels right for you."

"I'll do it."

"You will?"

"On one condition. If Nancy can convince Cal to sell, the money for the house has to actually be in your account before we give her our answer."

"Not a problem." A smile was in his voice. "Martin promised that once we sign the papers at the castle tonight, the money will be in my account by tomorrow afternoon."

She'd clearly heard the part about the money being in his account, but the other part about where he was signing… Had she heard him right? "Did you say you were signing the papers at a castle?"

"Yeah, I tried to convince Martin to link up here at my

office or even my house. But he's insisting we meet up at Fortune's Castle. He's been bugging me about seeing it."

Fortune's Castle? As a kid, she'd dreamed about the place. And Max didn't even want to see it? Eliza couldn't keep the excitement out of her voice. "Let me get this straight. You're going to the coolest place in town to sign papers and you consider that a problem?"

"Going there isn't the hardship, but Martin…he's a little eccentric. And he loves to talk. Once he gets started, it's one weird riddle after the other."

"He doesn't sound that bad to be around. He actually sounds kind of interesting."

"Interesting?" Max chuckled. "If that's the case, why don't you come with me to the coolest place in town?"

"Go with you to the castle?" The word *yes* almost leaped out of her mouth. "No. You're signing papers. This is important family business. I don't want to intrude."

"You won't be intruding. If I take you with me, I have an excuse not to hang around. I can tell him I need to get you back home. Please. You're my only chance of getting out of there before sunrise."

Fortune's Castle—how could she not go with Max to see it?

Chapter Five

Max pulled into the parking lot near the entrance of Vale Real Estate Group where Eliza was waiting for him. His office, located in a strip mall with five other small businesses, was just a few blocks away.

She got into the truck. "Hello."

"Hi." He waited for her to put on her seat belt then sped out of the parking lot.

While Main Street in Chatelaine was the definition of sleepy and vacant, the four-lane road running outside downtown that he merged onto was busy with late-afternoon traffic.

Most of the cars were headed in the opposite direction, probably destined for the GreatStore or the Saddle & Spur Roadhouse. If people weren't stopping at one of those two places, they were most likely taking the scenic route to Corpus Christi.

As Eliza settled more comfortably in the seat, a strange excitement he couldn't explain washed through him.

Every passing minute of the clock that afternoon, waiting for the time to pick her up to arrive had felt like ten. But it was worth the wait. She looked pretty and professional in a pair of stiletto-heel boots, black slacks and a mauve sweater.

She wouldn't need the extra jacket he'd tossed on the back seat. She'd brought a short, matching trench coat.

Eliza's phone buzzed in her purse, and she pulled it out. Engaged in sending text messages, she typed several responses. As she put her phone away, she chuckled softly and shook her head.

"Everything good?"

"Yes. That was just my dad giving me a hard time about ditching him tonight for a trip with you to the castle. My mom's away on business so he's, quote unquote, roughing it by himself."

"You had plans with your dad? I didn't mean to get in the way of that."

"You didn't. We were just going to eat leftovers in front of the television. And he's not complaining. Instead of heating up last night's chicken marsala, he's raiding my pizza stash."

"Pizza stash?"

"I like good pizza. I can't find what I want around here, so I make my own and freeze the slices. That way I can have it whenever I want."

"What kind?" She probably made the gourmet kind with toppings like basil and goat cheese.

"I make all kinds." Eliza shrugged. "But my favorite is sausage and pepperoni."

His heart leaped. Not that she had a reason to make him pizza, but he still liked the idea that they had similar preferences.

Max reached over to his phone in a holder on the dash and turned on the map app. "Thanks for giving up your evening to come with me."

"Thanks for the invite. And honestly, I should be thanking you for the opportunity to see Fortune's Castle."

"You were serious about really liking the castle?"

"Liking it?" She smiled. "I have a confession to make. From the age of five until I was about eight or nine, I used to dream about living there."

"Let me guess, as the queen?"

"No, my favorite stuffed unicorn, Pinky, was the queen. My teddy bear, Milo, was the king. I was their knight in shining armor sworn to protect them. When I wasn't slaying dragons, Lucy Belle and I would go on important quests to save the queendom."

"Lucy Belle?"

"My horse."

"Real or imagined?"

"Lucy Belle was very real." As Eliza grew more animated, a dimple fell deep into her cheek. "She was my neighbor's dapple-gray horse, and I was absolutely in love with her. But I'm sure if you asked my parents, they would say I was obsessed with her. I used to do extra chores around the house just so my parents would take me to see her. I cried for days when our neighbors moved away and took Lucy Belle with them."

"No wonder you know so much about horses. You grew up around them."

"I did. My dad is a farrier. He's semiretired now. When he wasn't traveling to a ranch or a farm, people would bring their horses to him. Having a horse barn on our property made it easier to do his job. And we temporarily took care of horses for owners until they could find permanent boarding."

"Does your mom work with your dad?"

"No. She's a logistics coordinator for an international aid group. But she loves horses. She has a palomino named Carpathia. She's in California on business, right now, and she checks in on her like a second daughter."

"Are you jealous?"

"No, but maybe I should be." Eliza laughed. "But it's hard not to love Carpathia, too. She's a beauty."

"You know, it's interesting you brought up boarding horses. In my teens during the summer, I helped out at the boarding stable that used to be south of Chatelaine. Mucking stalls, cleaning tack, grooming the horses."

"You mean Miller's Boarding Stable? I used to go there with my dad sometimes when they needed him to shoe a horse. We probably passed each other a few times."

"I don't know. I think I would have noticed a knight in shining armor riding a dappled gray horse."

She laughed. "Thankfully, by the time I reached my preteens, I'd given up my armor and my sword."

"Why thankfully? Personally, I think some of the dreams we have as kids are the best ones."

"That's an interesting way to look at it."

The road switched to two lanes and as he merged with light traffic, he could feel Eliza staring at him. He glanced over at her. "What?"

"Nothing."

"It's not nothing. You're doing that thing with your eyes."

"What thing? And why are your eyes on me and not on the road?"

Because it was hard for him not to stare at her. "You get this look in your eyes when you're thinking about something. It's your tell."

"Note to self. Never play poker with Max."

He's the one who would probably keep losing at cards if he played against her. His concentration would be shot the entire time. "What's your question?"

"It might be too personal."

"Why don't you let me decide that?"

"Well, I was actually wondering two things."

"Go for it."

"You're single and living alone. Why do you want a really large house?"

That was an easy question. "Growing up, I always wished for more space. There were six of us packed in a small house. My mom, four boys including me, and my sister. We're all two years apart in age. My sister was the only who had a bedroom to herself. My brothers and I had to double up. And there was only one bathroom. Things got pretty wild at times and there definitely wasn't any privacy."

"Let me guess. Your sister mostly hogged the bathroom. There were laundry mix-ups. Empty containers left in the fridge. Someone short-sheeting the bed. Maybe a few burping contests?"

"All of the above. Did you grow up in a large family?"

"No, I'm an only child, but my friend Tess grew up with four brothers in Dallas. Some of the stories she shared were outrageous." Eliza laughed and shook her head.

"After hearing her stories, did you feel lucky to be an only child?"

"I don't know. It might have been nice to have a younger brother or sister. But if they would have even thought about flushing the toilet when I was in the shower, there would have been a war."

A chuckle shot out of him. "Yeah, I did that a few times."

"Why am I not surprised?"

"Good question. Why are you not surprised?"

She circled her finger in the air. "That not so innocent look on your face, right now. It has trouble written all over it."

He laid his hand on his chest, mocking pain. "What? For your information I was a choirboy compared to my brothers and sister."

"Yeah, right."

Her laughter filled the truck and the place where his hand rested on his chest tightened with a jolt of happiness.

Max put his hand back on the steering wheel. "You said you had two questions. What's the second one?"

A few beats passed before she spoke. "What's it like to have a castle in the family?"

"I haven't really thought about it. It's a new thing and

I don't really feel connected to it other than Wendell Fortune built it, and he was my grandfather."

He'd managed to keep most of the resentment out of his tone, but from the quizzical expression on Eliza's face and her silence, he hadn't hidden it well enough.

As far as Max was concerned, Wendell had been a selfish bastard, and they were related in name only.

His grandfather's decision not to show up for his family had adversely impacted the Maloneys. If he had been there for his son, maybe Rick would have been a better husband and father. And Max, his mother, and his siblings could have had better lives before now.

As far as the inheritance, him and his siblings receiving money, or about to receive money, from Wendell's estate didn't change Max's opinion of him.

But would the money change him or his siblings? Max contemplated the question. Working in the financial profession, he'd heard stories from his colleagues of clients who'd become instantly wealthy and lost every dime. Or they'd kept every dime and didn't give a damn about other people. Like his grandfather had.

Sensing Eliza looking at him, waiting for an answer, snapped him out of his thoughts.

Eliza didn't need to know about his screwed-up family history. "Well, I'm sure you heard about me and my siblings not knowing we were part of the Fortune family."

"I heard a little about it."

"Finding out how we're related to them through my grandfather and that he left us money has been a lot to take in. Luckily, the man we're meeting at the castle, Martin Smith, is around to help guide us through the inheritance process. He was my grandfather's closest friend. When my grandfather died, Martin was granted control of the estate and my grandfather's affairs."

Max could feel Eliza's eyes on his face, and for the first time during the drive, he hesitated in glancing over at her. He'd just told her more than he'd ever admitted to anyone else, including his family. Maybe he shouldn't have.

She'd grown up fantasizing about quests and castles while he'd dreamed of just having a house with more room. What would he see in her eyes? Was she pitying him because she saw the money he was receiving from his grandfather as a handout?

"I'm really happy for you, Max. Once you sign the papers tonight, you'll be able to have the house you always wanted."

The sincerity in her voice released the tension that had just built up inside him. As it drained away, he momentarily met her gaze. "I found the perfect house because of you. Thank you."

"You're welcome."

He followed the instructions from the voice on the map app, instructing him to make the next right turn.

A narrow private road cut through the trees, and yards away a security gate stretched across it.

The castle sat in the distance.

A mix of apprehension and anticipation hit, and Max tightened his grip on the steering wheel. "We're here."

Eliza paused on the cobblestone pathway.

Pointed arches, flying buttresses and stained glass

windows adorned the decades-old, concrete structure. And were those… They were. *Wow!* Actual gargoyles.

As she tilted her head back to take in more, her heel caught on the edge of a cobblestone and she started to fall. Surprise sucked a breath out of her.

"Careful." Max caught her by the hand.

Off balance, she spun toward him. Her other hand landed on his chest near his shoulder, and he caught her lightly by the waist.

Max was so solid, and as always, he smelled wonderful.

Inches away from each other, their eyes met and seconds passed.

This was the closest she'd ever been to him, and touching him… Well, it was nice.

A glimpse of what she felt seemed to flash in his eyes. But it was gone so quickly, she wondered if she'd imagined it.

Concern showed on his face as he let her go. "You okay?"

Despite being saved from falling, she felt a little unsteady. "I'm fine. I guess I should pay more attention to where I'm walking." Eliza pointed at the structure. "This is so unreal. Your grandfather built an actual castle. Who in the world does that?" The question tumbled out of her mouth. "Wait. I didn't mean that in a bad way."

A chuckle softly rumbled from his chest. "I didn't take it that way. I have the same question. Maybe Martin can answer it."

"He's expecting you. We should go." As if Max didn't already know that.

As they walked up the incline, he moved slightly ahead of her.

Instead of polished lace up shoes, he wore sturdy, outdoor boots. Jeans encased his muscular-looking legs. A short, black, outdoor jacket made of a velvety-looking cloth stretched across his back and wide shoulders.

Her conversation with Tess came to mind. He'd dressed exactly as she'd envisioned him.

...the hotter they are, the more trouble they cause...

The biggest trouble she was having right now was keeping her eyes off him and not remembering how warm and solid he'd felt holding on to her a minute ago.

Eliza swiped the thought from her mind. She'd come along for the ride to see the castle, not fantasize about Max. So far, the castle did not disappoint.

They reached the large wooden door with an ornate brass handle and a circular knocker shaped like a lion's head.

He looked from the knocker in the middle of the door to the speaker built into the wall on the left. "Do you see an intercom button?"

"No. I guess you're supposed to use that."

Max looked to where she pointed. He raised the ring hanging from the lion's mouth and rapped it on the door.

A voice came through the speaker. "Hey there. Come on in. The door's unlocked."

Max's chest rose and fell with a deep breath. He pushed the door opened with his free hand, and the creaking hinges conjured up images in Eliza's mind of a lowering drawbridge.

They walked inside. Black and white tiles in a checkerboard design lay in front of them. An elaborate wrought-iron candelabra hung directly above.

Just like the outside, the grand entryway was an eclectic feast for the eyes.

A Byzantine-style mosaic of peacocks and birds covered most of the high arched ceiling, while several large paintings of medieval lords and ladies in outdoor landscapes sat high on the left side wall interspersed with torch-shaped sconces.

Farther down, Abbey bench seats and marble pedestals sat against the wall.

On the right, tall arches encased closed wood doors. Above the archways, stained-glass windows sat behind an interior balcony with an ornate gold railing. It also bordered the sweeping ruby-colored carpeted staircase yards in front of them.

They ventured toward the middle of the entryway. Three metallic sculptures of knights in armor on bended knee formed the bottom of a glass-topped table holding a large floral centerpiece. Wielding swords in their right hands, the knights' left arms were raised as if they were holding the glass up like a shield.

Max looked up. "Martin?" he called out.

"Up here." A gray-haired man with a short, bushy beard gave them a single sweeping wave.

"Do you want us to come up?" Max asked.

"No, I'll come down to you."

As they waited for the older man to meet them, Eliza

caught a glimpse of Max's apprehensive expression morph into a stoic mask.

A realization hit. Was this Max's first time in his grandfather's house? Suddenly, she felt nervous for him.

Eliza moved closer to Max and nudged his arm.

He glanced at her, blinking as if coming out of a haze. *You got this.* Eliza smiled at him, hoping he understood the message she was trying to convey.

Pulling back from wherever his thoughts had come into his mind, Max gave her a small smile.

Martin descended at a slow pace. His worn boots, brown pants and a long-sleeved tan sweater were at odds with the grandeur of the castle.

As he reached them, he smiled and opened his arms. It looked as if he'd planned to give Max a hug but then stopped short, extending his hand instead. "Glad you could make it. And you brought a friend."

Max turned toward her. "This is Eliza."

"Hello." She shook hands with Martin. "I hope it's okay that I'm tagging along."

"Of course it is." He patted her hand. "So you're the pretty lady Max was so worried about disappointing."

"Oh...?" Was that what Max had told him?

A hit of crimson tinged Max's cheeks. "Uh, yeah, Eliza came along because she was excited to see the castle."

"Really?" Martin's face brightened even more. "Then I have to give you a tour."

He gently tugged her forward, but Eliza held back. "Now? But don't you and Max have important things to discuss? I don't want to be in the way."

"Nonsense." Martin took a firmer hold of her hand and looped her elbow with his. "Our business can wait. Where should we start? The murals, maybe?"

The last thing she wanted was to get in the way of Max signing his papers. He'd been waiting to get the money.

She glanced over her shoulder at Max. *Sorry.* She mouthed the word to him.

Amusement filling his eyes, he mouthed back. *It's okay.*

"Come along, Max," Martin called out as he escorted Eliza toward the paintings. "There's a lot to tell about these murals. You'll want to hear it, too."

Chapter Six

Max paused with Martin and Eliza at the mural depicting a feast on a lawn outside a castle. But watching Eliza's face was the real draw. Her expression was a mix of genuine interest and excitement.

Martin pointed to the features as he explained them. "This painting has so many details. For instance, there are fifty people in the painting. That includes the lords and ladies, and the servants in the background. That number also equals the pomegranates on the table and in the baskets underneath. Pomegranates symbolize death and fertility. As you can see, the older lord slumped in the chair at the end of the table is much paler than the rest, and his eyes are closed. On the opposite end, there's a woman holding a small baby."

Eliza peered at the mural. "Mortality and life. I can

see it. But why the number fifty? What's so significant about it?"

As Martin stared at the mural, sorrow came and went from his face so quickly, Max almost missed it.

When the older man looked to Eliza it was gone.

"Lord Byron wrote a poem about the number."

He cleared his throat and began to recite it. "'When people say, "I've told you fifty times," / They mean to scold, and very often do; / When poets say, "I've written fifty rhymes,"/ They make you dread that they'll recite them too.'"

Was Martin about to go on a tangent citing a bunch of riddles, expecting them to guess the answers? Max tamped down his own sense of dread. *Please don't let this poem have fifty verses.*

"There's more to it." Martin turned and smiled. "A volume of poetry with that very piece is in the library. We can take a look at it after we look around upstairs."

Martin went on to give them a long-winded explanation about the other parts of the mural as well as the mosaic on the ceiling. "Notice the canaries in the trees by the peacocks. People often associate them being used in coal mines in the early days, but they were also used in silver mines as well. Did you know that, Max?"

"No. I didn't." And why would he?

"The canary theme carries over into the stained glass upstairs. Follow me, and I'll show you."

As Martin started leading them up the stairs, Eliza stifled a yawn.

Max tapped her lightly on the arm, and she looked back at him.

Stepping closer, he leaned down to whisper in her ear. Her perfume, wrapped in warmth, wafted from her skin. It took a beat for him to remember what he wanted to say. "The way he's going, we'll be here for fifty years. I know you're tired of listening to him. I'll get you out of the rest of the tour."

"Oh no, not yet," she softly replied. "He's really enjoying it. I don't want to hurt his feelings. Wait until after he shows us the stained glass."

"Everything okay?" Martin called down from the top.

Max leaned away to look at her. Humor and empathy shone in her eyes. "We're fine."

"Eliza, stay close to Max," Martin said. "The steps are narrow. They might be a little tricky to navigate in high heels."

Martin was probably being overly cautious. Still, Max stayed by Eliza's side, mirroring her pace.

As they grew closer to the top, he let Eliza walk ahead of him.

The dip of her waist and the gentle sway of her hips took him back to the pathway earlier when she'd practically landed in his arms. It had felt so good for her to be that close. He'd had to remind himself to let her go.

And she hadn't seemed to be in a hurry to move away. Or had he misinterpreted what he'd seen in her eyes?

As he stood with Eliza and Martin near the stained-glass windows, she chatted easily with the older man. Her eyes were so expressive. They were one of her best features. The tone of her voice was a close second. Melodic and smooth, like a cool, gentle breeze on a summer day.

His thoughts traveled back to the first time he'd met her. It had been at the real estate office. He'd been so caught up in her voice, he hadn't cared what she'd said. He'd just liked listening to her.

Eliza gently bumping his arm brought Max back to the present. It took a minute to process what her raised brow meant.

He cleared his throat. "Martin, we really appreciate the tour, but Eliza and I need to get going soon."

"Oh…" Martin's exuberance faded. "Of course you do. And here I am going on and on."

"But I loved hearing about the history of the castle," Eliza interjected. "Everything you mentioned was so interesting."

Martin's smile returned and he patted her arm. "Then Max will have to bring you back so I can show you the rest."

Downstairs, Eliza went to explore the library that was adjacent to the grand entryway.

Max preceded Martin into an office with a rug containing a black-and-silver design.

In front of them, a leather chair sat behind a large, polished wood desk. Behind it and on the wall to the left were floor-to-ceiling shelves filled with books.

A series of black-and-white photographs in silver frames hung on the other side wall.

Martin shut the door behind them. "I'm sorry getting this done has taken so long. Handling an estate of your grandfather's size involves a lot of bureaucracy."

He huffed in exasperation. "Bills, taxes, managing assets, lawyers' fees."

"I can imagine it's a lot to handle. I appreciate the time you spent settling the issues with me receiving the money."

"Glad to do it. I just need to review a few paragraphs in the document. In the previous one, Maloney was omitted from your name. They assured me the correction was made. I just want to make sure before we sign it."

Martin went behind the desk with a carved border with flowers around the top of it. He opened the middle drawer and retrieved a pen.

As much as Martin's modern appearance didn't fit with castle's ambience, he knew his way around the place. He must have spent a lot of time there with Wendell. From Martin's enthusiasm about history and lore, he and Wendell must have had similar sensibilities and the same quirky sense of humor.

But earlier, when Martin had been talking to them about the first mural, the older man's mood changed so abruptly when Eliza asked him about the significance of the number fifty. What was up with that? And then he'd skipped over explaining its significance.

On the day Martin had delivered the check to Linc during the family gathering, a couple of times, he'd switched the topic to something random when he'd been asked a couple of questions about Wendell in his last days. Instead of reciting a poem, like he had to Eliza, he'd told them a riddle instead.

Max drifted over to the photos on the wall. If Wendell were alive, would he be just as vague with his explanations or would he give honest answers about himself and the choices he'd made? "I wish I could ask him."

"What's that?"

He hadn't meant to say that out loud. Max hesitated. "I have questions I wish I could have asked Wendell."

"Like what?" Martin walked over to him. "I knew him well. I might be able to answer them."

As he sifted through the questions in his mind, two stood out. *Why did you abandon my father? Why did you let us all struggle financially when you had millions?*

Martin couldn't answer those questions and even if he could, it wouldn't change anything.

"Nope. I'm good."

"If you ever change your mind—"

"I won't."

"Well, if you ever do…" Martin looked away a moment, then gave him a small smile. "You've waited long enough. Let's sign these papers and get you your money."

Standing at the desk, Max signed the papers where indicated.

Martin stood beside him. "You and Eliza have to celebrate this. You're a lucky man to have such a wonderful, interesting woman in your life."

"I am very lucky to have her as my real estate agent." Max handed Martin the pen. "She worked hard to find me the right house." And she was going above and beyond to help him close the deal.

"You mean you two aren't…"

First Cal Pickett made assumptions about him and Eliza, and now Martin. "No, we're not together."

Martin scribbled his signature on the last page of the document. "That's too bad. You're buying a house. You should have someone to share it with. Your grandfather built this castle, and he was here alone. It was a sad situation. Never forget that money and things are not more important than people."

"Is this where you tell me money can't buy happiness?"

"Yes, that's exactly what I'll tell you." Martin closed the folder and set the pen beside it. "I know it sounds like a cliché, but it's true. If your grandfather were alive, I'm sure he would tell you the same."

If Wendell were still around, his grandfather would be the last person Max would want to hear that from. "It's easy to give that advice when you're rich. But I watched my mom struggle to raise me and my siblings because she didn't have enough money. And Linc, he basically had to sacrifice his own future to help keep things afloat. Trust me, we would have been a lot happier with Wendell's money back then, along with all of the things it could buy."

"I'm sure it was difficult." An anxious expression passed over Martin's face. "But I'm sure Wendell regretted that he wasn't able to help them more. But he was the type of man who believed in self-reliance. And that often comes from struggle. Wendell had to learn that the hard way. He grew up with great wealth and no consequences, and it wasn't till late in his life that he realized how much he lacked. For him, having all that money was a curse."

Martin's loyalty to his grandfather was admirable.

But it wasn't necessary for him to keep making excuses for Wendell.

"Well, I'm thankful to have some of that curse." Max extended his hand to Martin. "Thanks again for making it possible."

Martin shook Max's hand and lightly clapped him on the shoulder. "You have a good head on your shoulders. I'm sure you'll use the money wisely. Like maybe taking your Eliza to dinner as a thank-you for finding your house."

Max didn't miss the hint of mischief in Martin's eyes. "We should catch up with Eliza. She's probably wondering what's taking us so long."

Chapter Seven

Eliza waved to Martin as Max turned the truck around in the driveway.

The headlights of the vehicle illuminated the older man. Even though he smiled, she glimpsed sadness on his face.

As they drove away from the castle, she glanced in the side-view mirror. Martin still stood outside watching them drive away.

Suddenly, she felt sorry for him. "Is he staying at the castle by himself?"

"I think so. It's probably the most convenient place for him to stay while he's handling my grandfather's estate. Why?"

"It must be lonely for him. Maybe that's why he's so talkative."

"That could be. I know he's a lot to take. Thanks for hanging in back there."

"You make it sound like a hardship. I enjoyed meeting Martin and finding out about Fortune's Castle."

"Was it what you expected?"

"Yes and no. I anticipated the grandeur, but I was surprised by all of the symbolism and mystery. Your grandfather must have been a very interesting man."

"I guess. I wouldn't know since I never met him." Bitterness tinged his voice just like it had when he'd mentioned his grandfather on the way to the castle.

What was that about? Curiosity almost prompted her to ask, but it wasn't her business. The saying about money not being able to buy love seemed to be true when it came to Max and Wendell Fortune.

Max cleared his throat. "So, Martin made a good suggestion. He said we should stop for dinner. My treat. Kind of a mini celebration for finally getting the money. The Saddle & Spur Roadhouse is down the street from your office. If you're hungry, we go could there."

"I am hungry. Lunch seems a long time ago."

"Then it's a date." Max sat back comfortably in the seat. "Let's do it."

A date—like the two of them? No, he didn't mean it that way. What was she thinking? He just said it was a celebration for finally getting the money so he could buy the house. The house that in Cal Pickett's mind she and Max would occupy as a couple.

Apprehension tugged at Eliza. "Buying the house and pretending to be a couple—we should come up with a plan about how to handle that."

He glanced at her for a moment. "You're right. We should. But before we talk about us being a couple, can you walk me through the steps of buying the house?"

Eliza rolled her thought process back to step one. That's where they needed to start. This was Max's first time purchasing a home. "Because mortgages aren't involved on either end, it's actually straightforward. We'll work with a closing agency. They'll do a title search and make sure the property is clear of any liens or outstanding debts. They'll also prepare and review the contract and all the legal documents that need to be signed after that, handle your payment to the Picketts and the transfer of the property from the Picketts to you."

"How long will all that take?"

"That depends on everyone's schedules. A closing date is something we'll have to negotiate with Cal and Nancy."

Max tapped his thumb on the steering wheel. "So then you and I pretending to be a couple...we're probably looking at anywhere from two weeks to a month?"

A month? That was a long time to be in a fake relationship. "Maybe less than a month. Nancy seems to be in hurry to leave. But we really only have to pretend in front of Cal. Nancy said they don't spend time in downtown Chatelaine. They even shop in the next town."

"Then we just have to pretend when we're signing the papers?"

"Or maybe not even then." She shifted more toward Max. "You can sign them at a different time than Nancy and Cal. I'm sure she'll agree that the less contact we have with Cal the better. It will be less of a pain that way."

"Oh?" Staring straight-ahead, Max seemed to sink in the seat. "I didn't realize you viewed being in a fake relationship with me as painful."

He actually sounded hurt. *Crap.* "No, that's not what I meant."

"You don't have to walk it back. I get it. The less contact with me the better."

"No. You've got it all wrong. I want us to be in contact." *Oh great. That didn't sound weird.* "What I mean is—" Eliza stared at Max. The lights on the dash illuminated his face. She could see his lips were twitching. "You're messing with me."

Max's laughter boomed in the truck. "Yeah, I am. I couldn't resist."

Relief flooded through Eliza. "If you weren't driving, I would punch you."

He chuckled. "If you want to punch me when we stop, you can. But honestly, I agree. For everyone's sake we should make this closing as painless as possible."

During the rest of the drive, Eliza and Max talked more about the closing. They were on the same page about everything, including approaching Nancy with the idea of her and Cal completing the paperwork at the house with the closing agent.

They reached where they'd started from, and Max dropped Eliza off at the real estate office to pick up her car. After sending her father a quick text that she was going to dinner with Max, she drove to the Saddle & Spur Roadhouse.

Inside the casual restaurant, known for offering the option of a generous side of steak with every entrée, almost all the tables in the center of the dining room, and the booths lining the side walls were full.

After a ten-minute wait, the hostess standing at a podium near the dessert case led them to a booth and took their drink orders. Eliza and Max sat across from each other.

Max picked up two of the plastic-covered menus in a holder off to the side. As he handed one of them to Eliza, he glanced at a server hurrying past them carrying a tray laden with plates. "I guess everyone had the same idea about going out for dinner tonight."

"It sure seems that way. But the kitchen seems to be keeping up." As she started to peruse the menu, he barely glanced at his before putting it back in the holder. "You've decided already?"

"I already had an idea before we got here. It's lasagna night."

"You know the specials by heart? How often do you eat here?"

"Two times a week." He shrugged. "Maybe three. Don't judge me. Not all of us can make homemade pizza."

"No judgment. Honestly, if I didn't live near my parents, I probably wouldn't cook as much as I do."

"You must live pretty close to them."

"Just a few yards from the house I grew up in. I rent the cottage on their property."

"What's that like—renting from your parents?"

"It's good." Eliza mulled it over. She really hadn't thought about it. "We get to see each other on a regular basis, and we still have our privacy. Why do you look surprised?"

"Being in real estate, I just imagined you would want to own a house. Especially since you know where all the good ones are."

"Owning a house has it perks, too. I loved the house I owned in San Antonio, but I don't feel like I'm missing out on anything by not owning one here."

"You used to live in San Antonio and now you're here? That's a switch. Do you miss it?"

Eliza slid the menu back in the holder. "I miss having lots of stores, restaurants and movie theaters, and hanging out at the local spot with my girlfriends. And I was a lot busier selling houses."

"Do you think you'll ever go back?"

As her conversation with Tess came to mind, she hesitated. "I don't know. Anything's possible, I guess."

Their server, LeAnn, brought glasses of water and the sodas they'd ordered earlier with the hostess.

She took a pen and order pad from the front pocket of her apron. "Sorry for the wait. Do you have any questions about the menu or are you ready to order?"

"I think we're ready." Max pointed to Eliza. "Go ahead."

"I'll have the chicken breast sandwich and fries with ranch dressing on the side, please."

LeAnn smiled at Max. "Let me guess. The usual?"

"Yes, please."

"One lasagna special and a side of steak. Got it." She looked back to Eliza. "I almost forgot. It's not on the menu, but there's a special with the sandwiches tonight. You can have a side of steak or dessert."

Steak and a chicken sandwich was a bit much for her to handle. "I'll go with dessert."

LeAnn pointed to the plastic table tent near the menus. "The main choices are on one side. The hottie desserts are on the other, but we're almost sold out of those. But I'm sure that's not a surprise." She glanced at Max and then gave Eliza a conspiratorial smile before she walked off.

"Hottie desserts? What's she talking about?" Eliza reached for the table tent.

Max snagged it first. As he looked at it, he closed his eyes a moment. "No way. I can't believe they did this."

"Did what? And who's they?"

"The Chatelaine Fish and Wildlife Conservation Society. I'm in their Valentine's Day Bachelor Auction for charity. The restaurant and the conversation society made up a dessert menu to bring in more money for the charity and advertise the event."

Realization dawned, and Eliza barely stifled a chuckle. "Wait—you're one of the hottie desserts?"

"Kind of."

"Let me see it."

"Nope."

She grabbed it from his hand.

THE HOTTIE DESSERT MENU was written at the top of the card. Underneath it was a photo bubble with a head shot of Max wearing a black cowboy hat plus two other bubbles with photos of guys wearing the same. Next to each of the bubbles was a quote.

Eliza read the one next to Max's picture. "'I love hot apple pie and long walks in the rain.'"

He groaned. "I never said that."

"Isn't that a lyric from an old song? It was in the

movie *Guardians of the Galaxy*. Something about drinking piña coladas and getting caught in the rain."

"I have no idea." He shot her a shrewd look. "This is payback for me teasing you in the truck, isn't it?"

"Payback? Me?" Fighting back a smile, she feigned innocence. "That never crossed my mind. It really is a song. You should play into the lyrics at the bachelor auction. You could carry an umbrella, a drink and a pie. The bids for you will go through the roof." The laughter she'd been holding back bubbled out of her, and Max joined in.

He shook his head. "You're loving this a little too much for this not being payback. Just try not to laugh too hard at me during the auction."

"Oh no, I won't be at the auction. But my colleagues from the office and their friends may be there. What are you giving away? They might be interested."

He shrugged. "I haven't decided yet. I told the event coordinators it will be a mystery date. I'm leaning toward meeting for coffee and passing along a generous gift card."

"Oh...that's nice."

"Nice? That's it?"

"Going out for coffee plus a gift card is good."

"But..."

She was being judgmental. What he was offering really was okay, but... "Maybe offer something a bit more personal and specific like give them the choice of a coffee date or dinner. And instead of just a gift card, include a gift certificate for something like a spa day, and afterwards, they get a bunch of fabulous pampering products to take home."

"So basically you're saying I should make a little more effort."

She held up her hand and brought her index finger and thumb close together. "Just a tad. I'm only keeping your best interests at heart. As your totally committed fake girlfriend, I don't want you to look like a slacker compared to the other bachelors."

He glanced past her shoulder then back to her face. "'Totally committed' to being my fake girlfriend? Do you mean that?"

"Absolutely."

"Then trust me." He reached across the table. "Hold my hand."

Chapter Eight

Eliza frowned at his request.

Max managed to keep the smile on his face. Maybe he should have said please. But there wasn't time to say more.

She took his hand, holding tightly just like she had when he'd helped her up the stairs at the castle.

"You two look like lovebirds."

At the sound of another female voice, Max glanced back up. Nancy Pickett stood just beside their booth, smiling down at them, and Cal was near her side.

Max returned her smile. "Nancy... Cal."

Eliza's eyes widened a tad, but she smiled as she looked over at the couple. "Hello, you two."

Max gave her hand a brief squeeze and got out of the booth. "It's good to see you. I guess you decided to go out for dinner like we did."

Cal peered over his glasses at the dining room. "We did. But we didn't expect everybody and their uncle's best friend to be here tonight. The only seats left are practically in the bathroom or the kitchen."

"Oh, Cal, that's not true." Nancy swatted his arm. "The hostess is going to seat us at a nice table."

Cal huffed. "In the back. Up here, the seats are a lot roomier for two people...or more." He looked pointedly at Max and Eliza's booth.

Without missing a beat Eliza extended a welcoming hand. "Would you two like to join us?"

Nancy waved away the offer. "We couldn't. We don't want to interrupt."

"Young lady." Cal spoke to the hostess waiting for them. "We don't need a table. We're staying here." He pointed to the seat Max had vacated. "You slide in first, Nancy. My leg's a little cramped. I need to sit on the end so I can stretch it out."

As the couple got situated, Max sat next to Eliza. Should they mention the house?

But Nancy acted as if she didn't have a care in the world other than the menu. It was almost like they'd never had the conversation about persuading Cal.

Eliza had mentioned she wouldn't play poker with him, but if they were in a card game, Nancy would be the one to watch.

Cal's foot bumped into Max's "If you don't mind, I could use a little more space for my leg."

"No, problem." Max moved closer to Eliza.

As her thigh pressed to his, her warmth seeped into him. The memory of her almost falling earlier that evening at the castle flashed into his mind. The spot where her palm had landed near his chest still tingled.

Cal waved away the menu Nancy tried to hand him. "I know what I want. I'm having a T-bone. It doesn't make a bit of sense to come to a steak place and not have a steak."

LeAnn delivered Max's and Eliza's food, then took Cal's and Nancy's orders.

"Eat while it's hot," Nancy said. "Don't wait on us."

Hunger and a need for expediency prompted Max to dive in. Eliza had said the less time they spent around Cal the better. If he and Eliza finished eating before the Picketts, they could make their excuses and slip out.

But Eliza wasn't eating. She toyed with her fries.

Condiments… They weren't on the table. "The server forgot to bring ketchup for your fries, Eliza. I'll flag her down."

"No, not ketchup. She forgot the ranch dressing. I know it's strange, but that's what I like…" Eliza's gaze met his, and the look in her eyes reflected what he was thinking.

A good fake boyfriend would have already known that. He'd assumed the dressing was for her sandwich.

Feigning forgetfulness, he added, "That's right, babe. I'm sorry, I forgot ranch dressing is what you like on your fries now. Ever since you tried it at that place in San Antonio we went to, it's your new favorite thing."

Eliza released a faint laugh and shrugged. "What can I say? I'm hooked on it."

"That's strange," Cal mumbled.

"Nothing strange about," Nancy scoffed. "When we

first met, I used to eat Thousand Island dressing with everything. Remember?"

"Of course, I do." As Cal responded to her, he pinned Max with a direct stare. "I remember *all* of your preferences. That's important in a good relationship."

Max flagged down LeAnn about the ranch dressing She apologized and quickly returned with the condiment.

In between bites, Eliza asked. "So, how did you two meet?"

Nancy smiled but Cal was the one who chimed in. "We were introduced to each other by a lying cheat named Moby Prescott."

Nancy nudged him. "Cal, be nice."

"Why? It's true. He was a damn scoundrel."

"But it happened over fifty years ago. It really is time to forgive the man."

"Maybe I should." Cal crossed his arms over his chest. "Especially since Moby's loss was my gain." As he looked at Nancy, the scowl on Cal's face morphed into a teasing, affectionate smile.

The unexpected turn in Cal's demeanor took Max by surprise. Eliza tapping his thigh under the table made him realize his mouth was open and his fork was hovering in the air.

Nancy spoke to Eliza and Max. "In case you're wondering, Moby wasn't my boyfriend. He was a man Cal worked with. They were livestock inspectors."

"And he was a real character. He acted like he was a blue-ribbon-winning bull at a livestock auction." Cal peered at Max over his glasses. "Know what I mean, Max?"

"Uh...yeah, I think I do." Max forced himself not to look at the table tent, but it was like trying to ignore a needle poking him in the butt.

"You mentioned his loss was your gain," Eliza said. "Did something happen to Moby?"

"Sure did." Cal sat back in the seat. "He wrote checks his butt couldn't cash. You see, years ago, inspectors went with veterinarians to inspect the livestock before large-scale rodeos. Moby had been assigned to one that was happening outside Corpus Christi. But the day before the event, his fiancée from Dallas caught him dead to rights with another woman. He left to chase after her and I took his place. I walked into the arena and saw the prettiest woman there."

Nancy blushed as Cal took hold of her hand on the table. "I was the rodeo queen that year. Once I saw him, I could barely stay in my horse's saddle."

"So it was love at first sight?" Eliza asked.

"Yes." Cal and Nancy answered at the same time. They chuckled.

"That was fifty-six years ago." Cal squeezed Nancy's hand. "But it feels like yesterday."

"Aww, I love that." Eliza had a glowing, happy look on her face. "My dad feels the same way. He says being married to my mom has been like the best summer day and all the holidays rolled into one."

"That's so sweet." Nancy smiled. "How long have they been married?"

"Forty-six years."

As the three of them chatted about their families, Max focused on his lasagna and side of steak.

His parents' relationship hadn't been a good one. Rick and Kimberly had been forced into a shotgun wedding to keep up appearances after she'd found out she was pregnant with Linc.

Having more children had been too much for Rick. He'd walked out when Kimberly had been pregnant with Justine. The divorce papers had been delivered by courier.

The memory of being six years old, watching his mom cry as she read them, flitted through Max's mind. He didn't like seeing his mom upset but he'd been secretly glad Rick wasn't coming back. Witnessing his parents argue had been hell.

As part of his due diligence with the inheritance, Martin had hired a private investigator to locate Rick. As Wendell's son, legally he would have been first in line to receive the money.

The investigator had found Rick's second ex-wife, who'd revealed he'd gone missing about six years ago after they'd an argument. After that, the trail had led to California. Evidence there suggested he'd driven his motorcycle off a cliff and into the ocean. The wreckage of the bike washed ashore but his body was never found.

The bite of food Max had just taken suddenly tasted like ashes in his mouth. He washed it down with soda and waited for the conversation to turn to him. What could say? His dad had failed the marriage test, and so had his grandfather? Chances were, he would, too. That's why he was strictly catch and release when it came to relationships. Not the best thing to admit to his totally committed fake girlfriend…or Cal if he wanted the house.

Eliza's hand resting on his thigh pulled him out of his thoughts. He glanced at her and saw a hint of puzzlement and concern in her eyes. Giving himself a mental shake, he dialed back into the moment. He'd completely zoned out. The topic had already switched from marriage to Cal and Nancy's grandchildren.

Under the table, he laid his hand on Eliza's, reassuring her he was following along. She flipped her hand over and took hold of his.

Tension drained out of him.

LeAnn dropped off Cal's and Nancy's food. She glanced at Max's plate. "Is the lasagna not okay? Do want something else?"

"I'm good." He just needed to hold Eliza's hand a bit longer while he put the crap from his past back in the headspace box where it belonged.

"What's the story with you two?" Cal peered over his glasses as he pointed at Max and Eliza with his fork. "When are you getting married?"

"Well…uh…" Max swallowed not sure what to say. Eliza's hand tightening around his mirrored how he felt. Squeezed.

Eliza released a breezy laugh. "He and I have been going back and forth on this for a while. I'm leaning toward a year. Max would fly to Vegas tomorrow and tie the knot if I agreed."

A wry chuckle almost shot out of Max. She was way off the mark. He was leaning toward never.

Cal cut into his steak. "So you're not ready to get married, but you're moving in together. So I guess kids are pretty far off in the future, too."

Despite her calm demeanor, Max felt dampness on Eliza's palm. It was time to give her a break from the hot seat.

"We've talked about it." Max smiled and winked at Eliza, hoping to reassure her he now had the ball.

As he shifted his attention to Cal, genuine sincerity sobered his smile. "We both agree that raising a child is a huge responsibility. It's one of the biggest decisions a person can make, and it shouldn't be taken lightly. Everything you do, every decision you make can have an impact on your child's life and their future."

"And that's why we're waiting until we're ready." Eliza chimed in. Her tone was soft, but it mirrored his conviction. "And when that day comes, we'll be excited to welcome a child, maybe two into the world."

Staring into her eyes, Max could almost believe they were talking about something real. He'd never really stopped to seriously think about if he wanted children. And if he did, how many of them.

"Oh, yes, I agree." Nancy nodded. "Get there as a couple at your own pace and wait until you're ready. That's exactly the way to approach the decision of having children."

Thankfully, Nancy moved the conversation further away from marriage and children, settling on a variety of things from the sale of storage boxes at the Great-Store to the upcoming rodeo near Corpus Christi to the groundhog, Punxsutawney Phil.

According to Cal, the little guy had come out of his den and seen his shadow. Six more weeks of winter was on the horizon.

During the rest of the meal, Cal alternated between studying Max, then looking away, pursing his lips as if he was contemplating something. Maybe it was to not sell him the house.

Not knowing what thoughts were running through the older man's mind was unnerving. Max was never so grateful to see LeAnn pop by to pick up their empty plates.

"So have we decided on dessert?" the server asked. "Yours comes with your meal," she told Eliza.

Patting her tummy, Eliza declined. "I'll pass. No room."

"None for me either," Max blurted out. He just wanted to leave as quickly as possible. He was about to ask for the check when Nancy grabbed the table tent.

"Hmm, let's see what you have…" She perused the side with the regular dessert listing.

As light reflected off Max's photo on the hottie side, Eliza squeezed his hand.

What if Cal saw it? As Max thought of the possibilities, he broke out in a sweat.

Nancy pursed her lips. "I'm not sure if I want dessert or not." She leaned toward Cal with the menu. "Do you want something?"

Holding his breath, Max couldn't look away. The damn thing was like a train wreck about to happen.

Cal shook his head. "That T-bone filled me up pretty good. I'll skip it."

Nancy put down the sign. "I'm pretty full, too."

The release of Eliza's pent-up breath matched his own. She let go of his hand and reached for her water. If he wasn't mistaken, her hand was trembling slightly.

Max took out his wallet and handed LeAnn his credit card. "Make it one check."

"You got it." She left with his card and the plates.

"You didn't have to pay for our meal," Nancy said. "Thank you."

"It's fine by me," Cal interjected. "But buying me a meal won't persuade me to drop the cost of my house for you."

Was Cal saying what he thought he was? Max glanced at Nancy and she smiled and gave a subtle nod.

He looked Cal straight in the eye. "I stand by my word. Full asking price."

Cal studied him a moment, then extended his hand across the table. "In that case, you've bought yourself a house."

As Max shook Cal's hand, he matched the older man's serious expression, but inside he fist-pumped in the air.

Nancy beamed a smile.

Eliza nudged his shoulder and smiled. "Congratulations. You did it."

No. She did it. None of this would have happened without her.

On a wave of happiness and an impulse, Max leaned in and pressed his mouth to hers. Warmth and sweetness hit him all at once, and he lingered a bit longer taking it in.

He leaned away, and Eliza stared at him with her lips

formed in a soft "O." It took all his strength not to dive in for a more thorough kiss.

Nancy clapped her hands in excitement. "Oh, this is so wonderful."

Max gave himself a mental shake. What was he doing kissing Eliza at the table? He could say it was only to play up the act in front of Cal, but that would be a lie. Kissing Eliza had been an honest impulse.

The server stopped by, Max signed the bill and they all got up to leave.

"Gotta make a pit stop." Cal walked by the dessert counter. He paused. "Nancy, pick out a pie and we'll take it home and have it later for dessert."

She peered into the glass case. "Oh, they all look delicious."

Cal waved down the dark-haired woman behind the counter. "Excuse me. I'd like a pie to go please." He took out his wallet and handed the woman some money. "It's for my wife. Any kind she wants."

He started walking down the hall toward the restrooms, but then he paused, leaning his hand heavily on the wall.

Max and Eliza both took a step in his direction.

Nancy stopped them. "Give him a minute."

Long seconds later, Cal resumed walking down the hall.

"See? He's okay. It's the pain—it gets to him sometimes, and there's nothing we can do." Nancy's eyes grew bright with tears, and she gave them a wobbly smile.

"Oh, Nancy." Eliza laid her hand on the other woman's arm. "I'm so sorry."

Nancy patted Eliza's hand. "I'm the one who needs to apologize to the two of you. I'm sorry Cal and I blind-sided you tonight. If I would have noticed you when we first walked in, I would have made an excuse for us to walk back out."

"It wasn't a problem at all," Eliza said. "We enjoyed having dinner with you."

Max nodded. "I was hoping for a chance to talk with you and Cal. This worked out perfectly."

"Well, I appreciate you both." Nancy leaned in and whispered, "Especially, the kissing. If I didn't know better, I'd believe you two are for real." She went to the counter and ordered the pie.

Minutes later, Max and Eliza walked out of the restaurant behind Nancy and Cal.

Max noticed something. Eliza hadn't looked at him once since he'd kissed her. Was she upset at him?

The Picketts' SUV was closest to the door.

He and Eliza waited until the couple got inside.

Nancy was in the driver's seat. She started the car then opened the window. "Thanks again for dinner. Eliza, can you call us tomorrow? We'd really like to get things rolling on the sale of the house."

"Absolutely," Eliza responded. "I'll call you in the morning."

"Okay." Nancy waved. "Talk then." She backed out of the spot and joined the line of cars waiting to pull out onto the road.

Eliza's car was close by. An awkward silence hovered between them as they walked to it.

When then reached her sedan, she searched for her keys in her purse. "After I talk to Nancy, I'll call you."

"Works for me."

As she took out her keys, they slipped from her grasp and fell to the ground.

Max scooped them up. As he handed them to her, she gave him a quick smile that wasn't reflected in her eyes.

He couldn't let her leave with whatever this was between them. "Eliza, I'm sorry. I didn't mean to make you uncomfortable by kissing you."

"You didn't. You just caught me off guard. It was no big deal."

No big deal? Those last three words hit Max like an openhanded slap. It hadn't felt that way for him. He'd liked kissing her. And if she felt that way, why was she acting funny?

He should just walk away and deal with it. But the memory of how she'd looked after he'd kissed her flashed into his mind. He couldn't let it go. "So you're okay with kissing me?"

"Perfectly fine."

"Are you sure about that?"

"Why do keep asking me?"

"Because it doesn't feel that way. We'll have a hard time pulling off a fake relationship if you can't handle a kiss."

Her brows shot up. "I can't handle a kiss? Trust me, I can handle a good fake boyfriend kiss."

"And how exactly would you describe a good fake boyfriend kiss?"

"Are we really debating this?"

"We won't be if you answer the question."

Eliza faced him head-on. The light was back in her eyes. "One that doesn't catch me off guard." She was even prettier all riled up.

Max took a step closer. "Are you ready now?"

Chapter Nine

Though she said yes, Eliza wasn't ready for the feel of Max's lips on hers.

She'd thought the sudden rush that ramped up her heartbeat in the restaurant and the spark of sudden desire had been a fluke. But now she felt it again. She slid her hands up his chest and started to rise on her toes, wanting a deeper kiss.

The beeping of a car horn filtered in.

Eliza backed up and he let her go. "I guess that clears up any questions." The carefree laugh she strove for sounded breathless.

"I guess it does." The way he stared down at her made Eliza want to rush back into his arms.

But that was a bad idea. They were in a fake relationship to close the deal on a house. She couldn't lose her perspective.

She unlocked the car with her key fob.

Max held the door open for her. For a long beat, he stared as if he had something to say. She stood there, waiting for it. Then he just said, "Good night, Eliza."

"Good night, Max."

He shut the door after she got in, and as she put on her seat belt and started the engine, she willed herself not to look at him.

Tess was right. The hot ones were trouble.

During the drive home, Eliza almost called Tess as she sped past open fields and ranches. If anyone could help put her head back on straight about close contact with a client, she could. But Tess would probably ask if she'd been delirious when she'd agreed to be Max's fake girlfriend in the first place.

Miles later, she pulled off the two-lane road into the driveway leading onto her parents' three-acre property.

Up until two years ago, a ten-stable barn and pastures for horses had been on the land along with her parents' house and Eliza's cottage.

The barn, several yards from the back of the house, had been downsized to four stalls, but the land remained well-tended. Her father sometimes allowed people to temporarily self-board their horse in the pasture.

Up ahead, lights shone through the windows on the bottom floor of her parent's two-story home.

Her dad was still awake.

Instead of veering to the right where the driveway went to her cottage that was a short distance away, Eliza kept going straight. She parked in front of the garage on the side of her parents' house.

As soon as she walked through the front door, her father, Benjamin Henry, looked at her from where he reclined in a tan chair in the living room up ahead. "Hey, Lil Bit."

"Hi, Dad." Eliza shut the door behind her and dropped her purse and keys on a wood bench against the entry wall, along with her coat. She slipped off her ankle boots and walked in on stockinged feet.

Cool beige tiles transitioned to a plush beige area rug delineating the seating area in the room with gray, cream and tan decor.

Flames crackled in the light brick fireplace beneath the flat-screen television on the wall across from where her father sat.

Light from a lamp on a side table between the couch and her father's chair reflected faintly on his light brown shaved head. Dressed in loose red-and-black-checkered pants and a long-sleeved black shirt, he was ready for bed.

Leaning down, she kissed his cheek. The vanilla and bay rum beard balm he used wafted from his graying goatee. "Why aren't you watching TV upstairs?"

"Not the same without your mom." He patted her hand on his shoulder and the familiar calluses on his palm from years of working with horses pressed against her knuckles. "You okay?"

Her kiss with Max flitted into her mind, and her pulse leaped. "I'm fine. It's just been a long day."

"You sound like your mom. That's what she said during our video chat today."

"When's she coming home from California?"

"She's not sure yet. A transportation issue has come up. Call her when you get a chance. She wants to hear about your date." He rose from the chair. "I was just about to make some hot chocolate. Do you want some?"

"Yes. And it wasn't date. It was just an invite to see Fortune's Castle. Stopping for dinner afterward...well, it just happened." And so did the kisses? The memory of kissing Max flitted through her mind again.

"I know. You were chilling, hanging out or whatever your generation calls it. But for us old-school people, we call that a date."

As they walked down a small adjoining hallway, they passed a series of family photos on the wall. In an almost absent-minded gesture, he touched the gold framed picture of him and her mom.

She told him about the castle as they gathered ingredients from the pantry and the refrigerator. The ritual of preparing the mixture of unsweetened chocolate, sugar and milk was something they'd done together since she was a little girl.

As the mixture heated on the stove, he stirred it with a whisk. "I'd heard the castle was kind of an odd place. But when you're rich, I guess you can indulge in buying weird stuff. You said your client is one of the Maloneys that inherited money from the Fortunes?"

"Max Fortune Maloney. You might have actually met him years ago. He used to work summers at Miller's Boarding Stable."

"Maybe I did, but Miller's was a busy place back then." He turned the heat down under the pan. "But I do think I remember the Maloneys. When we first moved here, a group your mom used to belong to delivered food baskets during the holidays to families who were struggling. He has a bunch of brothers, right?"

"Three brothers and a sister." She took two mugs from an upper cabinet and set them on the black granite counter next to him.

"From what I understand, the father was gone, and the mother was raising the kids." Her father shook his head. "That was over twenty years ago. Sounds like things have really changed for them."

Max's comment about growing up in a crowded space came to mind. "Things have changed. Especially for Max. While we were at dinner, we ran into the owners of a house he's interested in buying. They're accepting his offer."

"Closing on another sale." He beamed a smile. "That's my girl. Congratulations."

"Thanks. It's exciting."

"Exciting, huh?" He turned off the stove. "I've never heard you describe a sale as exciting before."

She hadn't? "He's never owned his own home. I haven't worked with a client in that position in a while. Helping a first-time buyer find a home is one of the things that makes my job worthwhile."

"I'm glad to hear you say that." Her dad poured the steaming hot chocolate into the mugs. "It's good to know all that bragging your friend did about how fantastic things were going for her in San Antonio didn't drag you down."

Sunday night during dinner, she'd mentioned meeting up with Tess to her dad. "Tess wasn't bragging. She was just updating me on everything she's doing, since we hadn't talked in a while."

"The way you described the conversation, sounded more like bragging to me. Why else would she feel the need to rub it in about how successful she is?" He took mini marshmallows from a bag on the counter and dropped a few in each mug.

Eliza dunked the marshmallows with a spoon. She paused as he squirted a dollop of whipped cream from a can into her drink. To her father, it probably did sound like Tess was bragging to her, especially since she'd left out an essential part of their brunch chat.

Continuing to let her dad think that way about Tess was the equivalent of throwing her friend under the bus. "Actually, she was telling me all that because she was offering me a job."

"And what did you tell her?" Her father's face settled into a neutral expression.

"She asked me to think about it. I didn't want her to think I didn't appreciate the offer, so I agreed."

He picked up his mug. "That's it? You're just thinking about it?"

"Don't worry, Dad. I'm not going anywhere." She clinked her mug to his. "We have a lot more hot chocolate dates ahead of us."

"And what about nondates to the castle with the Fortune Maloney guy? Any more of those happening?"

As Eliza sipped her hot chocolate, the warmth of the drink on her lips reminded her of Max's mouth on hers. Desire, delicious and sweet, curled through her middle.

No. Remembering that kiss was a bad idea. She

couldn't let herself indulge in any more nondate kisses with Max. Good thing the chances of that happening were slim to none since they didn't have to see each other for a while.

Eliza topped her hot chocolate with a little more whipped cream. "The only date that's happening with Max is on closing day."

The sooner that happened the better.

A soft dinging sound entered Max's dream. It didn't matter to him. Eliza did.

He was kissing her again in the parking lot of the Saddle & Spur Roadhouse. But this time, he was *really* kissing her in the way he'd wanted to...no holding back.

Last night, it had taken a huge effort not to pull her closer so he could feel her soft curves against him... but now, in his dreams...

The drumming sound of the 8:30 a.m. alarm on his phone yanked him fully awake.

Sun streaming in from the slats of the blinds on the side wall of his second-floor bedroom made him shut his eyes again.

Damn...

Lying on his stomach, Max squinted as he reached over and snatched the phone from the wood bedside table. He didn't have to be in the office until ten. He could snooze for another few minutes. But Max tapped "stop" on the screen instead of snooze, the promise of coffee teasing him more awake.

A message bubble caught his attention. That's what

the dinging sound had been earlier. *A deposit has been sent to your account...*

Turning over on the mattress, he sat up and threw back the navy sheet and comforter. Sitting on the edge of the bed in his blue boxer briefs, his heart rate ticked up as he tapped the bubble, enlarging it to the full message.

A grin took over his face. It was from the estate lawyers.

Jumping to his feet, Max fist pumped in the air. "Hell yeah, I'm a millionaire!" Or at least he would be by the end of the business day. Close enough.

His phone rang with a call.

As Max answered, he snagged a pair of black-and-white athletic shorts from the bottom of the bed and put them on. "Martin, hey, I was just about to call you..."

Well, maybe not, but he would have eventually.

"Good morning. You sound pleased. I guess you know about the upcoming bank deposit?"

"Yeah," Smiling, Max raked back his hair with his hand and then rubbed the back of head. Even though he knew the money was on the way, it felt unreal. "I just received the message. Thanks again for making it happen."

"Happy to do it. Like I said before, I know the standard advice of don't spend it all in one place and use it wisely doesn't apply to you. You're an expert at handling finances. What I will say is make time to enjoy it with someone special. Maybe Eliza fits in that category?"

Receiving the money and being able to finalize closing on the house did provide another opportunity to invite her out. And have a chance to kiss her again for real instead of just in his dreams.

That possibility made Max smile. "I'll definitely consider it."

"Good. I'm sure you have plans to make. If you ever need to call me...well, you know how to reach me."

Why would he ever need to call Martin? The inheritance was straightened out. "Okay...thanks. I appreciate that."

"Again, I'm happy for you. Goodbye, Max."

"Thank you. Bye."

Excitement hummed Max as he ended the call. He couldn't keep the news to himself. Who should he tell? Eliza?

Calling to tell her he was a millionaire might sound like he was bragging about it. He didn't want her to think he was full of himself.

Max pulled up the message app on his phone. He'd tell his brothers. More than anyone, they would understand how important receiving the money was.

He sent out the text.

Coop responded first.

That's what I'm talking about. Congrats.

A second text immediately came in from Linc.

Congrats. Next round of beers is on you.

Max texted back a reply.

Thanks. Next round of beers on me—definitely.

After making a pit stop in the adjoining bathroom, Max left his bedroom and walked down the beige carpeted steps of his condo.

Just as Max rounded the corner and walked into the kitchen with light-colored wood cabinets and white counters, his phone rang in with an incoming video call from Damon.

He answered it and his dark-haired brother's face appeared on screen. Damon was in his car.

"Dude, congrats!" The youngest of the Fortune Maloney brothers flashed a smile.

"Thanks." Max took a coffee pod from a box in a top cabinet.

"Did you just get back from a workout?"

"No, I just woke up." Max walked farther down and stuck the pod and mug in the Keurig on the counter near the fridge. "I'm getting ready to go to work."

"Work? Are you serious? Once I get my money, I'm kissing my bartending job at the Chatelaine Bar and Grill goodbye." Damon leaned closer to the screen. "You can do or go anywhere you want, right now. You could literally book a flight, go to the airport and be at a beach somewhere by noon." His smile widened and mischief shown his brown eyes. "I can't wait to do that."

While the coffee maker did it its thing, Max took a box of Cheerios and a bowl from the nearby cabinets. "And that's why you're coming to talk to me as soon as you get your money."

Damon laughed. "You worry too much. You should be thinking about how lucky you'll be at the bachelor auction next week. Now that you have money, all the women will be bidding on you."

As Max took a carton of milk from the refrigerator, the memory of Alana from the GreatStore staring at him, popped into Max's mind. If that's the type of attention he was facing from the audience… "Yeah, I'd be willing to pass on that."

"You need to lighten up, show up and just have fun with it. That's what me and Coop plan to do. Anyway, I better go. I gotta run some errands before my shift starts. Talk to you later."

Max rested back against the counter. He munched on his cereal and enjoyed his first caffeine hit of the day.

Beyond his modestly furnished living room with a flat-screen on the wall, he could see his back deck and yard through the sliding door. The conversation with his youngest brother replayed in his mind.

The thought of Damon with millions in his hands was scary and Coop wasn't far behind. Coop always leaped into things before he looked, and Damon went through life as if being a responsible adult was an option, not a requirement.

Yeah, reining both of his younger brothers in was a priority. Just like they were teaming up to have fun at the auction, once they received their inheritances, they'd collaborate on some harebrained, expensive adventure.

And the whole, quitting his job thing… Damon needed to think smarter than that. It was fine if he wanted to quit bartending, but it was the perfect time to consider something bigger. Like he was thinking of doing.

Max put his empty bowl in the sink. He was branching more into financial planning. Expanding into something investment based with someone was on his radar, too. But that was in the future.

The only major change involving finances he was making now was his address. And maybe he would take Martin's suggestion seriously and celebrate with Eliza. Maybe a nice dinner somewhere out of Chatelaine once the closing on the house was completed.

The earlier excitement Max felt when he first woke up to the best news of his life returned. He looked forward to all of that happening. Soon.

Chapter Ten

Eliza followed a group of women across the parking lot to the back room entrance of the Saddle & Spur Roadhouse.

Would you mind doing me a favor?

Helping with a client. Opening the office early. Working an extra weekend. That's what she'd imagined Reggie was going to ask her to do when she'd stepped into her office earlier that day. Not spending her Tuesday night attending the charity bachelor auction.

But Reggie had reserved an entire table and had planned to attend with a few friends. Sharon was going to be there, too, with her friends. But Reggie and her group had to cancel, and she'd asked Eliza to fill a seat and hand over a check to the Chatelaine Fish and Wildlife Conservation Society.

Eliza took her place in line behind three women chatting and laughing among themselves.

One of them, a blonde, wore a pink jumpsuit and sky-high stilettos. The curvy blonde next to her was killing it in a low-cut black shirt and black jeans. The other woman, dark-haired with a flawless brown complexion, looked cute and confident in a beige floral boho dress and tan cowboy hat.

Eliza gently tugged the end of her navy lace bell-shaped sleeve from under her bracelet. Good thing she'd gone home to change out of her work clothes. Her sweater, skinny jeans and ankle boots were the right mix of dressy and casual.

The blonde in the jumpsuit flipped her hair over her shoulder. "I hope this will be worth emptying the dollars from my piggy bank."

"Dollars from your piggy bank?" The dark-haired woman gave the blonde a raised brow stare. "I have questions. First of all, you do realize this is a charity event and not a strip club?"

The blonde with the piggy bank gave a slight eye roll and smiled. "Yes, I do realize that. Despite what you believe, I do know how to act in public. But who knows—if things start to get boring, throwing a dollar or two at the bachelors might liven things up."

"Or get us kicked out." The curvy blonde chimed in. "And then we'd lose our chances to win a millionaire."

"Chances?" the piggy bank blonde asked. "There's more than one?"

The curvy blonde nodded with a knowing smile. "Three of them. Alana, this woman I work with, said…"

The three women huddled closer and spoke in lowered voices so that Eliza couldn't hear what they said.

But she easily guessed which three bachelors they were talking about. Max and his two brothers. She'd heard they were part of the event, too.

Be honest with yourself, that's not how you found it...

Okay, she didn't just hear about it, she'd peeked at the Chatelaine Fish and Wildlife Conservation Society's website. She been avoiding Max, except for text messages and phone calls. It was a way of establishing boundaries. Ones that had almost been forgotten with their kiss in the parking lot. They were in a pretend relationship, not a real one. And she was just helping him buy a house.

Still, she couldn't fight the urge to see his face, even if it was just a photo on the CFWCS website page. His had been there along with the rest of the bachelors and their bios that pointed out three key things about them.

Max's had mentioned he was good with numbers as an accountant and financial adviser, and good with his hands, as in, handyman repair skills (wink, wink). In the Friend's Report section of the bio according to those how knew him, he was generous. The one to call when you need someone to bail you out of or help fix a problem.

From what she knew about him—she didn't know if he was good with his hands. But when they'd reviewed the summary purchase costs for the homes he'd been interested in Max had easily calculated the numbers.

And the way he'd advocated for them to help Nancy and Cal Pickett did show a high level of generosity.

Even without the draw of his inheritance, Max was

a catch. He and any of the three women in front of her would make a really cute couple.

A small hint of jealousy hit at the prospect, and Eliza swept it away. Whoever Max walked away with wasn't her concern.

Her involvement with him started and ended with him moving into Cal and Nancy's house. And if all went according to plan, it would happen soon. The attorney had emailed the contract yesterday to the older couple for them to sign. Once that was done, they would be one step closer to closing.

And Nancy was in hurry to get it done. She'd already packed up most of the house and scheduled the movers.

Just like the kiss, this charity auction was for a good cause, too, and she was there to fill a seat.

The line moved forward, and a short time later, Eliza reached the beige-tiled lobby. A large colorful sign on an easel showcased a photo collage of various fish and wildlife. It also had a graphic of a cowboy hat and lasso interwoven with the slogan *Save the Environment—Lasso a Cowboy*.

Eliza handed her VIP pass and Reggie's check to the woman sitting at the check-in table.

"Thank you for supporting the Chatelaine Fish and Wildlife Conservation Society Valentine's Day Bachelor Auction." The woman beamed a smile as she wrapped a pink plastic glow bracelet around Eliza's wrist. "Have fun."

Eliza entered the room.

Laughter and conversation mixed with modern country music reverberating from speakers in front of a DJ table in the far corner. A raised stage with a short center runway took up most of the right-hand side.

Opposite the stage, guests stood in line in front of the two portable corner bars and mingled around a long table with event-themed T-shirts, hats and other items sold in support of the charity auction.

The rest of the guests were at the buffet table or seated in the middle of the space at round tables covered with black and white tablecloths with crimson and pink accents.

Eliza spotted Sharon's reddish-blond curls across the room. She was sitting with two other women at a table near the stage.

As she reached the table, Sharon spotted her. "Hey, you made it. I was wondering if you were still at the office."

"No. I left a little early, but I had to go home first."

As Eliza settled into chair next to Sharon, the office manager pointed around the table to a pretty brunette with tanned skin and a rosy-cheeked woman with short dark hair. "These are my friends from Corpus Christi, Lois, but we just call her Lo, and Desiree. Everyone, this is Eliza."

"Hello." Eliza returned the women's smiles.

"So what's your lucky number?" Lo, the brunette, ask her.

"My what?"

Desiree pointed to a paddle on the table in front of Eliza. "Your number is on the back."

Eliza picked up the paddle with a picture of a Great Blue Heron that sat on top of an event program. She flipped it over and surprise made her pause. "Fifty."

Not that she'd need the number or the event program. She wasn't planning to bid, and she'd already made an online donation to the society.

As Desiree set her empty wineglass aside, one of the restaurant staff working the event picked it up. "We should probably get refills on our drinks and some food before the auction starts."

Everyone agreed, and Eliza and Desiree were picked to go first.

On the way back from the bar and the buffet, Eliza heard a familiar voice. "Hey, Alana…"

One of the women who'd been in line in front of Eliza earlier stood nearby talking to a blonde in a red dress.

Eliza set her small plate of food and glass of merlot on the table and sat down. As she munched a steak and cheese bite, curiosity needled her to peek at the program. The same picture of Max that had been on the hottie dessert menu was in the beginning pages. He was bachelor number two.

Alana said…

What *had* the blonde told her coworker about Max and his brothers?

No doubt, there were more than a few rumors circulating around the room about the brothers and their money. The bidding for the three of them would probably get out of control.

And the woman who won Max… What if she and Max really hit it off? He'd have to explain the house and the fake relationship situation. If she were in the woman's shoes, she wouldn't be crazy about the situation. Maybe he would console the new woman in his life by letting her help him decorate his new house.

As she thought about Max sharing all the firsts he'd experience in his new home with some yet to be named woman, the food she'd just eaten sat in her stomach like a rock.

No. Eliza set the program aside and picked up her wine. She didn't need all that nonsense rolling around in her headspace. She didn't care who won Max. Their dating relationship was fake. Only their business relationship was real, and that had nothing to do with whatever happened tonight.

Eliza took a long sip of wine. Her phone chimed and buzzed in her purse with a text. She took it out and read the message.

Win me.

Great. Text spam. What company or pervert was bothering her now?

Just as she went to delete the message, she glanced at the number where it came from. *Max?*

She glanced around but didn't see him. He was probably bored somewhere, waiting for the event to start, and was sending her funny text messages to pass the time.

Eliza sipped wine and texted him back.

I think you sent this to the wrong number. I don't enter strange contests.

Max answered immediately.

I know exactly who I'm texting. You, Eliza. You have to bid on me and win.

She didn't have to do anything…unless she wanted to. But why not have some fun with him?

Sorry. I'm passing on the hottie dessert menu tonight. But I'm with a table of women who might be interested.

Max quickly replied.

I don't want them. I want you.

A hit of happiness wrapped itself in the heady warmth that came with her next sip of wine. She really should just tell him no, but…

If I were to do as you asked, what would I get in return?

Dots appeared in a text bubble and then his message appeared.

A lot more than a gift card.

"Excuse me." The Saddle & Spur server slipped past Max and the bachelor in front of him to walk out the open double doors into the event room.

He glanced at his phone, impatient for Eliza to reply to his message.

Whoever had decided the large storage space should double as a staging area for the servers working the auction and a holding area for the bachelors hadn't thought it through. It wasn't just crowded, it was hot as hell.

Max adjusted the black cowboy hat on his head and tugged at the collar of his black Western shirt, wishing he could untuck it from his jeans. He and the other bachelors were dressed like cowboys to match the theme.

But he couldn't be too critical when it came to making bad decisions. He hadn't considered all the angles when he agreed. Like he flat out just didn't want to be there.

A blue-ribbon-winning bull at a livestock auction...

At dinner the other night, he'd told Cal he'd understood what he meant, but he really didn't...until now.

But there was a clear way out of the situation. Eliza would bid on him and win, and he'd pay her back with interest if she wanted him to.

Just as he went to text her more details, Coop clapped him on the back. As a ranch hand, he looked at home in his brown cowboy hat, chambray shirt and jeans. "The place is packed. You ready?"

He was ready for anything that would get him out of there. "Yep. Where's Damon?"

"He's around here someplace cuttin' up or flirting with someone. Who knows with him?"

A middle-aged woman who was one of the event organizers raised her voice to get everyone's attention. "Bachelors, it's time to get ready. And put away your phones."

Coop clapped Max on the back again. "Good luck out there."

"Same to you."

"Don't need it." Coop grinned as he took his place in line.

It was time to go onstage, and Eliza still hadn't answered him. He took another look at his cell, as if simply wishing it would make her reply text appear. *Damn.* The event organizer gave Max a pointed look. He stuffed his phone in his pocket.

A dark-haired woman outfitted like a cowgirl took the stage. She was an entertainment news reporter from Corpus Christi. "Hello, everyone. I'm Vicky Chandler. Welcome to the Chatelaine Fish and Wildlife Conservation Society's second annual Valentine's Day Bachelor Auction!"

Applause and cheers erupted from the crowds as the Big & Rich classic tune "Save a Horse (Ride a Cowboy)" thumped through the speakers.

The bachelor procession onstage was welcomed with even louder applause as they lined up on the back part of the stage.

Vicky smiled at the audience. "In the short time the CFWCS has been in operation, this volunteer force has worked tirelessly to ensure we're living in harmony with our environment through their youth educational programs, wildlife research grants and other vital conservation efforts. And tonight, we're focused on what could be considered one of the most endangered species on the planet. The bachelor."

Chuckles rumbled around the room.

The MC continued the introduction, then invited the president of the society onstage.

A weird feeling like he was being watched made Max scan the crowd.

His gaze collided with a blonde in a red dress. The woman from the GreatStore. What was her name? Ah. Alana.

The collar of his shirt suddenly grew more constricted as a feeling like an oncoming tornado came over him.

Everyone knows your track record with women ain't the best.

Coop's words reverberated in Max's mind along with the worst-case scenario. What if Alana bid on him and won?

As he glanced away, he spotted Eliza in the crowd.

She was staring at the screen of her phone. Was she wondering what he meant by his last message? He should have been more specific. He should have just told her the truth. She could have anything she wanted if she just got him out of this.

Eliza started texting…but his phone wasn't buzzing in his pocket.

She got up from the table, headed for the exit.

Who was she messaging? Where was she going? When was she coming back? Max started to sweat.

"All right, ladies, it's time for the part you've all been waiting for…" Vicky Chandler paused dramatically as the DJ played a drumroll. "Let's lasso some cowboys!"

Chapter Eleven

As Eliza walked out the door into the lobby, she reread the text from Nancy

Cal saw Max. He doesn't want to accept the offer now. HELP!

Eliza dialed Nancy's number and the call picked up on the third ring.

"Eliza, thank goodness."

Nancy's desperate tone raised concern. "Nancy, I don't understand your message. Cal saw what about Max?"

"The pie I bought at the restaurant after we had dinner—I kept the plastic bag it came in. Cal needed a bag for something and when he went to use it, there was a flyer with a menu and an announcement about a bachelor auction. It had Max's picture on it. Now Cal's convinced that either the two of you aren't together or that Max is up to the same thing Moby Prescott was when he cheated on his fiancée."

Oh crap... "Nancy, this isn't what it seems."

"So Max isn't in a bachelor auction?"

"He is, but—"

"Oh…" Defeat filled Nancy's voice. "Cal said if that's the case, he won't sell. He doesn't care how much money we'll lose if we back out of signing the contract now."

This couldn't be happening. They were so close to completing the deal. "But the bachelor auction is a charity event. That's all it is. If you put Cal on the phone, maybe I can explain it to him."

"No. It won't matter what you tell him. Cal is old-fashioned. The way he sees it, if Max is with you, he's not a bachelor and he shouldn't be in the auction. And Max taking some other woman out on a date means he's stepping out on you. And Cal said he won't sell his house to someone he calls a 'low-down, dirty scoundrel.'"

"Max isn't stepping out on me because—" She paused and drew in a shaky breath. "Look, Nancy, everything will be okay. Trust me." Eliza rushed to the door leading into the event room.

"But how?"

"I can't explain now, but I'll call you back. Soon." As Eliza disconnected the call and crossed the threshold, the crowd cheered.

"Whew! We're kicking things off with a bang. That was intense." Vicky mimed wiping sweat from her brow. "Congratulations to lucky lady number eight. Head over to the hitching post and claim your cowboy."

Smiling, bachelor number one left the stage.

"And now, ladies, our next bachelor. There are way too many reasons to count why you'll want a date with him. Come on up here, Max Fortune Maloney."

Cheers filled the room, as he joined Vicky in the middle of the stage.

He was already up? Eliza wove through tables and chairs, hurrying to get back to her seat.

She put the mic in front of him. "All of the women bidding tonight are dying to know, what's the date you're offering?"

Max leaned toward the mic. "Uh…one big surprise, I guess."

"Well, that sounds mysterious. And I know the women in this audience love big surprises. Let's get things going with an opening bid."

As Eliza sat down, Lo made an opening bid.

A second later, another woman shouted out a bid from somewhere in the room. Then another.

Shoot! Eliza searched in front of her on the table. Where was that darn paddle?

Sharon tapped her arm and leaned in. "Everything okay?"

"My paddle—have you seen it?"

Sharon pointed. "It's under your plate."

Eliza snatched it up and stood. *I can't believe I'm doing this…* She threw up her paddle and entered the bidding fray.

The back and forth between the MC and the women in the crowd made it hard to keep up. But as the bid crept higher, one by one, women started dropping out.

But the woman in the tan cowboy hat who'd been in line with her friends outside was in it to win it. She steadily outbid Eliza and the remaining contenders.

Soon, only Eliza, Alana, Lo and the woman in cowboy hat were left.

Alana topped the next bid, but Eliza went higher.

Alana glanced back at her.

"Dang," Sharon murmured. "If looks could kill…"

The woman in the cowboy hat sat down and tossed her paddle on the table in defeat.

"I'm out." Lo gave Eliza a look of appreciation and teasingly bowed down in respect. "Go ahead, queen. You got this."

But Alana wasn't giving up. She got to her feet, shouting out an amount that made Eliza pause.

She looked to the stage and the MC stared down at her expectantly. For the first time since the bidding started, Eliza met Max's gaze. He appeared cool and calm, but one of his hands was balled at his side, and his smile was tight.

He won't sell the house to Max now.

I need your help.

The remembered defeat in Nancy's voice just a minute ago echoed in Eliza's mind, along with the determination in Max's voice the day he'd first seen the house. She had to finish this. For Nancy and Cal. And for Max.

Eliza raised her paddle high, shouting out a number that raised oohs and aahs of shock from the crowd.

Alana dropped down in her chair.

The MC pointed to Eliza. "Aaaand sold to lucky

number fifty with the winning bid! Ladies, thank you for the enthusiastic bidding. Especially the lady in red."

I won... Adrenaline drained out of Eliza and her legs almost gave out. She sat down in a heap.

Everyone at the table and people nearby congratulated her.

Sharon leaned in and tugged on her sleeve. "Did you hear what the MC said? You need to go to the hitching post and claim your cowboy."

"The *what*?"

"The table with the stanchions around it on the other side of the room." She pointed it out.

Eliza headed in that direction.

On the way, the woman with the beige cowboy hat and the women at her table called out. "Congratulations, lucky number fifty."

Eliza smiled her thanks. Hopefully her luck hadn't run out. If luck were currency, the amount she just bid on Max should have more than covered it.

Onstage, Vicky Chandler continued with the auction.

"Ladies, welcome our next bachelor to the stage, the notoriously single Cooper Fortune Maloney! Yes, that's right, ladies. He's one of the Fortunes of Texas. Let's hear it for this cowboy who promises you one wild ride!"

The crowd erupted in applause as Max's brother walked on stage.

At the hitching post table, Eliza handed over her credit card and paid the smiling woman sitting behind the table.

The bidding for Cooper started, and Alana was constantly throwing up her paddle to counter the other women's bids. The action was almost as fast and furious as it had been for Max.

Why was Alana being so aggressive? Either she was a true fan of the charity and was helping drive up the bids, or she really wanted to win a date.

Once the transaction was complete, she turned to leave and smacked into a familiar hard chest.

As Max held her by the shoulders, he looked happy, relieved and slightly dazed. "You bid on me. When you didn't answer my text and I saw you walking out, I didn't think you were going to. Thank you."

"Don't thank me yet."

Shouting grew louder as the rapid-fire bidding for Cooper drew closer to an end with Alana and only a couple of other women involved.

"I didn't hear you." Max leaned in. "What did you say."

"And sold to the lady in red!" Vicky Chandler pointed to Alana and the audience cheered.

Eliza took Max's hand and pulled him out the room and into the lobby. She told him about her call with Nancy.

He closed his eyes a moment and shook his head. "I had a feeling this auction was a bad idea. So in Cal's book, I'm neck and neck with his favorite lying cheat Moby Prescott. But you won me. That should make a difference, shouldn't it?"

"There you two are." One of the conservation society's volunteers for the event walked out of the room with a photographer. "You can't slip away yet. We need a photo. Get closer and smile."

Eliza stared up at Max. A thought flitted through her mind. It probably fit in the "bad idea category" along with him being in the bachelor auction.

Rising to her toes, she clasped her hand to his nape and kissed him.

Chapter Twelve

As Eliza drove away from her cottage, she glanced at her parents' house.

No one was home. Early that morning her father had sent her a text telling her they'd have to skip their usual Saturday morning coffee together. He'd gotten a call from someone he knew near Corpus Christi who needed help with their horse. He would be gone until Sunday.

His plans fit in with her schedule. She was holding down the office for the weekend along with Sharon.

Honestly, it had been a relief not to have to face him again. Lately, things between them had been...tense.

That past Tuesday, the night of the Valentine's Day bachelor auction, the gossip train had traveled faster to her parents' house than she had. And her father had done something he hadn't done since she was in high school. When she'd arrived home after the auction, he'd been waiting for her on the porch with the light on.

Desperate gold digger or a secret possessive girl-friend—those had been the two rumors he'd heard about why she'd entered a bidding war for Max. Her dad had been worried about her reputation.

She had to tell him the truth. The whole truth. The homeowner's stipulation on the sale, the pretend relationship, the frantic phone call from Nancy and finally her desperate bid and convincing kiss. He hadn't approved, but he'd also said that since she was a grown-up, he was staying out of her business.

After their talk, and her mom's "just checking in" call that ended with a subtle warning to be careful, she'd felt anything but a grown-up. But she'd made choices, including kissing Max for a photo that had now been plastered on every blog connected to the conservation society and Chatelaine. But it served its purpose. The capturing of that moment, and suggesting her winning Max was part of the plan, was enough to convince Cal to get back on board with selling Max the house.

She regretted the kiss. Not because the photo was plastered on the internet. But because she just couldn't forget the way his hands had slid around her waist to hold her close. How she'd naturally leaned into him. How the firm press of his mouth caused decadent desire to curl through her like wisps of smoke, clouding her mind and making her forget where they were until Max had eased away.

It had been less than a satisfying ending. But ever since that night, she wanted to kiss him again. Was it possible to become addicted to kissing him? Thank goodness she wouldn't have to tempt fate. The closing attorney had the ball now and would finalize the house transaction. If she and Max did have to be in the same room, kisses were off-limits for them from now on.

And once she got past her fake relationship with Max, she was never doing anything remotely close to pretending with any man again.

Close to a half hour later, Eliza walked into the real estate office carrying her work tote.

Sharon looked up from where she sat at a desk in the middle of the space, safeguarding the hallway behind her. "Good morning, Eliza."

"Good morning." Eliza slowed her steps, anticipating Sharon to update her on the day or hand off a few messages.

Sharon focused on typing a document on her computer screen.

"Any messages?"

"Nope, nothing." Sharon offered up a shrug. Her cheeks flushed with a huge smile. "You can just look forward to a really good day."

"Okay…great." As Sharon kept smiling at her, Eliza smiled back.

A day without appointments wasn't what she'd call a good day. But maybe Sharon had something special going on in her life that put her in such a good mood.

Eliza walked down the hall and into her office.

The reason for Sharon's smile quickly became apparent.

Max.

He got up from the chair in front of her desk and walked toward her.

Eliza's heart kicked up a beat. Which one did she like better? Business casual Max? Cowboy Max? Super casual Max in a pair of jeans, boots and a long-sleeved, aqua pullover like he wore today? Who was she kidding? He looked good in everything.

She cleared away the thought. "What are doing here?"

"Hello to you, too."

"Hi—I'm sorry." As he walked toward her, Eliza went behind her desk and set down her tote. "I'm just surprised to see you. We didn't have a meeting about the house scheduled for today, did we?"

"We didn't." He held her gaze. The shirt he had on turned his eyes a deeper shade of blue. "You've been avoiding me."

"No, I haven't."

Max ambled behind the desk and stood beside her. "I've invited you for coffee, lunch and dinner this past week. You've turned me down every time. Is something wrong?"

Something was very wrong. Between his gorgeous eyes and the shape of his kissable mouth as he formed words, it was hard not to just stare at him. Dropping her gaze didn't help. The way his shirt molded to his chest made her want to touch him. She hadn't experienced any of these problems around Max before the bachelor auction.

Eliza conjured up a smile as she took her laptop out

of her tote. "No, nothing's wrong. I'm just busy. We've got a lot going on this weekend."

"No, you don't."

He must have heard her talking to Sharon. *Great.*

The chime on the front door rang.

On the monitor, she spotted two people walking in.

She was saved. Eliza reached for the pen and pad on her desk. "New prospects. I should go greet them."

Reggie strode past the door, walking toward the reception area, and Eliza did a double take. Reggie was supposed to be off today.

"You don't have a lot going on here at the office because I asked Reggie to give you the weekend off."

"You what?" Good thing Reggie knew about the fake relationship. Otherwise what would she think about Max's request? Another realization kicked in. "And she agreed?"

"Yes. I told her I've been trying to thank you for all the hard work you put in finding my house. But you've been too busy to meet with me."

"You shouldn't have done that."

Max slipped the pen and pad from Eliza's grasp and set them next to her laptop. "Will you please just listen to me? What happened at the auction has made things weird between us. If I could turn back the clock and fix it so the moment never happened, I would."

Here she was fantasizing about kissing him again, while Max wished their fake relationship hadn't happened. Period. Reality hit her like a splash of cold water in the face.

As she moved to take a step back, Max took hold of

her hand. He sat back on the edge of the desk. "I know you said we're even because I paid you back the money you bid on me, but I still want to treat you to the date you won. I want to take you someplace where we don't have to deal with the stress of people wondering about us because of the auction, and we don't have to pretend to be anything. We can just be two people having a good time. Let me do that for you. Please."

Maybe stress *was* the problem. Trying to please Cal and Nancy and then the auction. Now, everyone she ran into lately seemed to know about the bidding war she went through to win Max. And she could tell by their faces they were drawing all the wrong conclusions. No wonder she was on the brink, fantasizing about things between her and Max that weren't true.

Next week, the house would close, and their ruse would end. They really did need to talk about how to make the shift from fake relationship to the next logical step. Friends.

Embracing resignation and a solid plan, Eliza smiled at him. "So hottie bachelor number two, exactly where are you taking me to have piña coladas and pie in the rain?"

"I'm not telling you." Max's slightly mischievous grin went straight to his eyes. "You'll have to come with me to find out."

Eliza stepped out of the back seat of the town car parked in front of the high-rise luxury hotel in downtown Dallas. Max got out behind her.

Chauffeured cars, a private jet, Max had gone all out for the surprise weekend getaway.

He smiled and took her hand. "Ready?"

At his touch her heart ricocheted in her chest. The champagne she'd enjoyed during the flight and her excitement over the weekend, that's all it was. With the house about to close, they were in the friend zone now. Lots of friends held hands.

She smiled back. "Yes."

They walked into the elegant marble-tiled lobby, a bellman in a burgundy-and-black uniform in tow with their luggage.

Before leaving town, they'd swung by her cottage, and she'd packed an overnight bag. She'd also changed into a sage-green sweater, beige pants and boots. After all, she was flying high with a gorgeous millionaire. She should try to look the part.

They paused at the concierge station, and Max gave his name to the dark-haired woman in a burgundy blazer behind the desk.

The concierge beamed a customer-friendly smile. "Welcome, Mr. Fortune Maloney. We've been expecting you and your guest." She opened a folio, pointed out the card listing the hotel amenities and other important information.

As Max had told Eliza on the plane, they were staying in a large suite that had two separate bedrooms.

The woman handed the folio with the key card to the bellman as she spoke to Eliza and Max. "Your private concierge, Yvette, is waiting for you upstairs in your suite. But any of the concierge staff is available to as-

sist you day or night, for anything you need. Your bellman will take you up now. I hope you enjoy your stay."

"Thank you."

As the bellman walked ahead of them, clearing the
way through the semicrowded space to the elevator,
Max murmured to her, "A private concierge? This place
is more impressive than I realized."

"Impressive" was now at his fingertips. But it would
probably take some time for him to get used to it. "I've
never stayed here before. Who recommended it to you?"

"One of my clients on Lake Chatelaine."

In other words, one of his wealthier clients.

Would he become part of that crowd now, not thinking twice about buying expensive things or taking luxury vacations?

On the plane she'd asked him if he had any other big
plans for the money, outside of buying the house and
this trip. Other than buying his mom some new furniture to outfit the house his brother Linc had purchased
for her, and making sure she had money to treat herself to whatever she wanted, he didn't have any special
plans at all.

But getting a taste of experiences like staying in this
hotel could change him.

What was that quote she'd read in a magazine once?
Was it Henry Ford that said it? Something to the effect of money merely unmasking a person instead of
changing them.

What would Max's newfound wealth reveal in him?
Would he remain the thoughtful generous person he
was, or would he change?

But why was she getting wrapped up in Max of the future? Right now, he was the guy she enjoyed being around, and he was treating her to a weekend that had been wonderful so far.

They passed by a small boutique where a peach-colored cocktail dress caught her eye.

She froze. In her haste, she'd packed some cute outfits, but she'd forgotten to pack a nice dress. *Shoot!* Max had mentioned they were going someplace fancy for dinner, but he wouldn't say where. Another surprise.

"Do you want to go inside and take a look?" Max tipped his head toward the boutique entrance. "You still have time buy a few things before your spa appointment. My treat."

The offer to treat her to a shopping spree was so tempting, but this felt like a place to draw the line in accepting his generosity. She wasn't going to take advantage of him. And if she did let him buy her clothes, every time she put one of the garments on, she'd remember he'd bought it for her. That felt like a little too much baggage for a dress. No, she'd find time to come back on her own.

She nudged the handles of her purse closer to the crook in her arm. "We should go up to the suite first. We probably shouldn't keep Yvette waiting."

Eliza and Max were the only guests in the elevator with the bellman. He swiped the key card and put in a code on the keypad that would only allow Max and Eliza access to where they were staying.

The elevator went higher and higher still before the doors dinged open.

The walked out into a private entry. Two dark-wood console tables with lamps and tall ceramic blue vases with white flowers bracketed the doors.

They walked through the open double doors into an expansive carpeted living room area with sumptuous furniture in shades of cream, bronze and blue. An elegant polished wood table with a floral centerpiece and four padded chairs sat in front of one of the large floor-to-ceiling windows framed by navy drapes.

Every window had an impressive view overlooking the city.

A uniformed woman entered the space. "Hello. I'm Yvette, your personal concierge. Where would you like for us to put your luggage?"

"Are both areas the same?" Max asked.

"Yes, they're identical."

He looked to Eliza, giving her first choice. "I'll take the one on the right," she said.

As the bellman delivered their luggage to the appropriate bedrooms, Yvette pointed to a kitchen with a dark granite breakfast bar and high-backed stools. "I have champagne and peach mocktail mimosas ready. May I pour you a glass?"

Eliza considered the choices. She should probably back off the champagne for a while. "I'll have a mocktail please."

"I'll have one, too," Max said.

Yvette went to the kitchen and a short time later she reappeared with their drinks in crystal champagne flutes.

As Max made a toast, his blue-eyed gaze held hers. "Here's to the perfect weekend."

Eliza clinked her glass with his. "To the perfect weekend."

Their first with no obligation to pretend to be anything but what they were to each other. Just friends.

Yvette pointed out a few key amenities and how to reach her. She also reminded Eliza about her spa appointment before she left.

Eliza went to her area. The bedroom and attached bathroom were equally as luxurious as the rest of the suite.

After changing into a fitted white tee, a mauve sweatsuit with a zippered top and her not-for-workouts tennis shoes, she peeked in the leather-covered resource book by the bed and found the info about the spa located on the top floor.

Max had mentioned she was getting "the works." The premium package consisted of a massage, a coconut salt scrub, hot towel steam with aromatherapy, a mani-pedi and bottomless mimosas or iced tea.

Anticipation made her a little giddy as she tossed a few essentials along with the key card into a small zippered pouch. She still needed to run by the boutique and find a decent dress. The one in the window had definitely caught her eye. Hopefully they had it in her size and it wouldn't cost her a chunk of the commission she'd just made on Max's house.

What was he going to be doing while she was getting pampered? Hanging out in front of the television? Touring Dallas? He hadn't said.

Eliza walked out of her room carrying the pouch and her jacket.

At the same time, Max walked out of his bedroom shirtless, in a pair of sea green swimming trunks carrying a towel and a shirt.

Hard biceps, solid pecs, rows of endless abs grabbed her attention. The happy trail and the V-cut in his lower abs prompted her to drop her gaze to where it led.

Warmth tugged in her middle and her breasts grew tight.

Eliza dropped her gaze again, encountering his muscular legs. Even his feet were perfect in a pair of black flip-flops. But the V and the happy trail practically called her name, and she stared at where they pointed.

Was the slight bulge in his trunks growing larger?

She shouldn't look. She couldn't stop looking.

Her nipples tingled, and Max's gaze dropped to her shirt.

Yep. The girls were waving at him.

Their gazes met. His expression reflected what she felt.

Speechless, hot and bothered, and aroused.

Three things you shouldn't be experiencing in the friend zone.

As if they'd both hit upon that conclusion at the same time, she slipped on her jacket and headed out while he quickly put on his shirt.

Heat flushing through her cheeks, she got into the open elevator. "Enjoy your swim," she called out.

"You, too," Max called back. "I mean—"

The doors to the elevator shut, cutting him off.

Maybe she needed a swim to cool off. She'd have to settle for the next best thing. Washing away that memory of Max in a really large bottomless alcoholic mimosa.

Chapter Thirteen

Max tossed his black suit jacket on the sectional in the living room area of the suite and adjusted the open collar of his gray button-down shirt. He was ready for their seven-thirty dinner reservation. Sort of.

Laps in the pool and a long shower still hadn't cooled him off. He kept reliving the moment when he and Eliza stepped out into the living room earlier.

The way she'd looked at him, it had taken every ounce of his strength not to walk over to her and kiss her until they were both out of breath. But if he'd done that, he would have broken his word to her about what this weekend was about. Two people having a good time. And from the way she'd been avoiding him, sleeping together wasn't part of that definition. And that was okay. He'd missed her coming back from her spa appointment and didn't get a chance to let her know that wasn't the expectation. Just because they had a physical attraction didn't mean they had to act on it.

He just needed to make sure every part of him and not just his brain got that memo loud and clear.

Max went to the window by the table and stared at the busy street, many floors below. He really just wanted Eliza to enjoy herself and to feel appreciated for everything she'd done for him. If she would have let him take her shopping, he would have done that, too.

But when Yvette had delivered the dress from the boutique while Eliza was still at the spa, she'd told him it was already paid for. He'd had to settle for buying her a pair of earrings.

The saleswoman at the boutique had remembered Eliza and the dress, and helped him pick a pair that went with the outfit. He hoped she'd wear them tonight.

The door to Eliza's room opened and she walked out.

The saleswoman had said Eliza had tried on the dress in the window, but that Eliza's second pick had been the perfect one for her.

The navy midthigh, sleeveless dress was simple in design. But it clung to her curves in all the right ways, and the slightly flared skirt, paired with her strappy stiletto sandals, showed off her gorgeous long legs.

Eliza had piled her hair into a bun and soft, curly tendrils hung near her cheeks. Her eyes looked even more expressive framed by long lashes. And her lips... The cherry color she painted on them made her mouth look even more luscious and tempting.

She'd need a coat. Too bad he couldn't wrap his arms around her and keep her warm.

As she walked over to him, he couldn't stop staring. "You look gorgeous."

"Thank you." Eliza gave him a slightly shy smile, and both of her dimples sank into her cheeks. "And thank you for the spa appointment. I really enjoyed it."

"You're welcome." He almost forgot. "I have something for you." Max went to his jacket and took the jewelry box out of the pocket. He handed it to her.

She opened it. The teardrop-shaped earrings with tiny beads interspersed with sapphire, ruby and diamond chips sparkled in the light.

Eliza released a soft gasp. "These are from the boutique... I wanted them, but they were too expensive. Max, you shouldn't have."

She'd noticed the earrings. No wonder the saleswoman had pointed them out as the ones he should buy.

On a reflex, Max reached up to cup her cheek. He stopped himself before he raised his arm, and balled his hand closed. "For me, treating you is not about the money. I just..." He couldn't find the words to explain.

"I understand. You're just paying me back for everything."

He shook his head. "No." Max reached for her arm but bumped her hand instead.

The box flipped and the earrings fell.

Eliza looked down at the navy carpet. "Where'd they go, I don't see them."

"They're probably under the table." He dropped down to look. The earrings weren't there. Max got to his knees.

"But that's so weird. They couldn't have gone far.

Wait. I think I see them." She pointed. "They're just under the edge of the drapes."

"Got 'em." He snagged the earrings. As he turned back around, he smacked his forehead against the wooden leg of one of the chairs. Sharp pain dropped him back on his butt, and the earrings fell from his hand.

"Max…" Panic filled her voice as she went to her knees in front of him. "Are you okay?"

Stars and her face swam before his eyes, as he held his hand against his throbbing forehead. "Yeah, I'll live."

"Let me see. Did you cut your head?" Moving closer, she took his hand away. "I don't see any blood, but you have a red spot. Are you dizzy?"

Her perfect breasts were inches from his face. As he breathed in her wonderful perfume, want struck him hard and he groaned.

"What is it?" Eliza cradled his cheeks in her hands and looked into his face. "What can I do?"

"You could kiss it better." The words slipped out.

Eliza blinked, staring at him. A moment later, she leaned in and pressed a soft kiss to his forehead. "Is that better?"

"No." Honesty seemed to be the consequence for bumping his head.

She kissed the spot again. "What about now?" The warmth of her mouth feathered his skin.

Max released an unsteady breath. "You need to go lower."

"Here?" She kissed the tip of his nose, then looked at his face.

He met her gaze and saw desire reflected in her eyes. "Lower."

Eliza pressed her mouth to his, soft lingering kisses that melded into one long press of their lips.

Max swiped his tongue along the seam of her mouth, and as she opened to him, Eliza rested her hands on his shoulders. He took hold of her waist, and she followed his lead, straddling him as his tongue drifted over hers and hers drifted right back.

He glided his hands up and down her back, bringing Eliza closer. Her dress rode high on her thighs, and the heat of her seeped through the front of his slacks. Max pressed his erection against her, and he swelled larger.

She undulated her hips over him and hunger rose. He was no longer dazed by pain but with need. Nothing else mattered but holding her, kissing her, having her. If it were possible to drown himself in her, he would.

Max slid his hands to the top of her back and found the tab of the zipper on her dress. But he forced himself to pause, focus on her face and breathe.

"Eliza, if you don't want more than kissing to happen, I'm okay with that. But if that's all you want, we need to stop now."

Eliza knew what she wanted.

She wanted to stop pretending that she didn't want to be with him. To stop fighting attraction. There would be consequences, but she'd deal with those later.

She reached for the top button on his shirt and flicked it open. "I don't want to stop."

Max released a harsh breath, and she met him halfway, welcoming the hard press of his mouth and a hungry kiss.

He broke away from her mouth to sweep kisses over her cheek. "Not here. I want you in my bed."

The husky tone of possession in Max's voice caused desire to unfurl deep inside her.

She got off him and they stood. As they rushed past one of the couches, one of her stiletto heels caught on the rug and she nearly stumbled. Max swept her up in his arms and carried her the rest of the way.

By the time he set her down by his bed, she was burning from his fiery kisses and heated caresses. Eliza tore open the buttons on Max's shirt and he slipped it off. The muscles in his torso rippled, and the V cutting along his hips deepened, framing his abs. Wanting to see the rest of him, she unfastened his belt buckle and the top of his pants. She tugged at his zipper.

But that's as far as she got. Max trailed kisses down the side of her throat and unzipped her dress. He glided the straps of her dress down her shoulders, and she shimmied it down her hips. It fell down her legs and puddled at her feet, leaving her in a skimpy blue lace bra and matching bikinis.

Max took a small step back and stared at her.

She'd picked out the scraps of lace at the hotel boutique at the last minute while buying the dress. She'd picked them out for herself. She liked fancy lingerie. But from the look on his face, she'd made the right choice for him, too.

The sweep of his gaze down and back again made

her breasts grow heavy and desire pool inside her. Her legs went weak and threatened to collapse.

Max fit his hands into the curves of her waist. His eyes never leaving hers, he backed Eliza to the bed. "You were beautiful in that dress and you're even more stunning out of it."

He followed her down to the mattress, and as her back hit the surface, he covered her body with his. Max's kisses down to her breasts left tingles in their wake. As he closed his lips around her nipple, he sucked it into the warmth of his mouth. Trailing his fingers down her belly, he slid his hands past the lace barrier covering her sex and slowly dived in.

Eliza arched up. Caught in a surge of ecstasy, she sighed out a rushed breath. "Max…"

After a long tender kiss, he eased away from her. As Max took off the rest of their clothes, anticipation made her heart beat against her rib cage. She couldn't wait to feel all of him, skin-to-skin.

After finding a condom, he came back to her and fit himself between her legs. Quick, shallow thrusts became one, deep wonderful glide in.

They moved in sync. Giving pleasure. Seeking pleasure. And, ultimately, finding it…together.

Later on, as she spooned back against him, the consequences she'd set aside suddenly reared back. Unease started to pool in her middle.

Max held her tighter. "You're thinking about something. I know it. What is it?"

She forced a carefree chuckle. "You know? You can't

see my face. You don't know if I'm doing that thing you say is my tell."

"But I'm right." Max kissed the back of her shoulder. "You're thinking hard about something. And I know it's about us. We're done with the pretending, remember? So tell me."

Knowing Max, he wasn't going to accept "nothing is wrong" as an answer. "Well, you mention pretending and that's the thing. One minute, we were pretending but just in front of Cal. And then we were pretending in front of everyone, but we were kind of leaning toward just friends, and now we're what? How do we even explain it to people?"

He rose up and leaned on his elbow, turning her on her back. Taking one of her hands, he threaded their fingers together. "First of all, we don't have to explain anything to anyone. It's none of their business. And second, as long as we understand what we're doing and what we want from each other, that's all that matters. You just asked what we're doing. Let's figure it out."

Her stomach unexpectedly growled in response.

Max laughed and kissed her bare belly. "I guess the first thing I should do is feed you. We missed our reservation, but we can still get dressed and go somewhere. Where do you want to eat?"

"I'm fine with ordering room service from the restaurant here. When I was glancing through the hotel's information guide, I saw the menu. It looks good."

"Let's eat here, then." Max reached for the guide next to the bed and found the menu. "Order whatever you want. Nothing's off-limits."

Did that include him, too, even back in Chatelaine? That possibility sent a surge of heated desire through her.

Max studied her face and his mouth tipped up with a whisper of a sexy smile. "I don't plan on starving you, but I can only take so much. If you keep staring at me like that, we won't be eating dinner tonight."

"But feeding you is probably a good idea." She slipped the menu from his hands. "I wouldn't want you fading out on me because of lack of energy."

He chuckled and shook his head. "All right there, Miss Snappy Comeback."

Wrapped in each other's arms, they looked at the menu together. They kept it simple, ordering chicken and salmon entrées. They decided to split a piece of chocolate cake for dessert.

When the food arrived, they sat at the table by the window in the living room area, wearing nothing but the plush hotel robes. They shared their meals with each other.

Max offered her some of his broccoli spears. "Back to your question. What are we doing?"

"Whatever it is, it needs to be enjoyable not stressful like our fake relationship was." She cut off the florets part of the spear and ate them.

"Agreed." He snagged the stalk she left behind from her plate and ate it. "What does that look like to you?"

"Good question. But I already chimed in one thing. It's your turn."

"Well, I think we shouldn't rush to define it because

other people might want us to. Let's take it one moment, one day at a time."

Eliza wasn't sure she liked the way that sounded. "Are you saying that you don't want us to be exclusive?"

"No, that's definitely not what I mean. I'm just saying there's no need to rush through the stages of a relationship. Let's just focus on getting to know each other."

"So you're suggesting an 'exclusive, no strings, let's get to know each other while enjoying time together' kind of relationship?"

Max nodded as if reviewing it in his mind. "Yeah, I think that sums it up well."

"Honestly, it sounds like you're not willing to commit to anything. Where does a relationship like that lead us or is this a relationship at all?"

"I want to be in a relationship with you." He reached across the table and took her hand. "I'm just saying let's be cautious because I know of people who've rushed into things before taking time to get to know each other. And it didn't work."

"Sometimes it does. My parents knew they wanted to be together after a month. Cal and Nancy were in love at first sight."

A troubled look passed over his face, and he let go of her hand. "It worked out for them, but it didn't for my parents. Staying together and then breaking up made life harder for everyone. Some people aren't made for long term commitments or maybe they just don't believe in them enough to commit."

Eliza could tell it was a tender subject, but she needed to know. "Does some people include you?"

"I don't know. With the things I've witnessed with my family…" Sadness came and went from his eyes. "A part of me wants to believe that it's possible."

She'd never doubted that love and forever were possible. Sure, relationships could be hard. That's where things like communication, patience, wanting the best for each other, and laughter were key. Along with love. Those were qualities she'd witnessed in her parents, and in Cal and Nancy's relationship, too.

Eliza wanted so badly to share her point of view. To convince him that that the right person, love was possible. But she was getting ahead of herself. They weren't in love.

And if all he'd experienced were the bad things in his family with love and long-term commitments, it made sense that he would approach relationships with a healthy dose of caution.

Approach with caution, that's what she'd have to do now if she agreed to the arrangement. They did want the best for each other. And laughter as well as patience with each other were there, too. They would have each other's time, but love might not ever enter the equation for him. Was she okay with that?

Eliza weighed her options. Pushing the whisper of doubt aside in her mind, she reached across the table and laid her hand over his. "We know where we stand on long-term relationships. We have differing opinions. I think that highlights something we need to keep at the top of our list."

"What?"

"Communication. So we can avoid misunderstandings."

Max laughed. Seeing her puzzled reaction, he added. "No, communication is a good one. I'm laughing because the day of the open house, Cal was so adamant about it, but he wasn't always the easiest guy to communicate with. On the other hand, under all the gruffness, I got the sense that he really cares about people."

"You really liked Cal, didn't you?"

"I did. But respect is more like it." Max's expression grew thoughtful. "He's the solid, family type, the type who'd never let you down."

Had someone let Max down in the past. His father? Another important male figure in his life?

He focused on Eliza again. "So…basic communication. Tell me something I don't know about you."

"I'll tell you but only if it's a trade-off. And if we ask each other specific questions."

"Q & A, kind of like a game. I like how you think. Okay, first question—what's your all-time favorite food?"

"Pizza," Eliza replied.

"That's what I thought."

"So why did you ask?"

"It's good to be certain before you ask a question."

Not a stretch since he worked with numbers.

Now that they were done with their meals, Eliza removed the clear plastic from the plate with the slice of chocolate cake. She set it between them on the table.

Good thing they only ordered one. It was almost large enough to feed three people.

She took a bite. Chocolate and a hint of coffee drifted over her tongue. "Now it's my turn. What made you want to become a financial adviser?" Ooh, wait. Maybe she shouldn't have asked that question considering his family background. He'd said things had been tough for them.

He took a bite of cake and relaxed back in the chair a moment. "I'm a natural for it. Well, my mom clipped grocery coupons to save money. While my brother Linc kept my younger brothers and sister in check so she could get the shopping done, I would help by managing the coupons. I could always calculate what was the best buy." With his fork, he lopped off another bite of cake. "My turn. Have you ever lived or worked outside of Chatelaine?"

"A couple summers, when I was in high school, I visited my aunt, uncle and cousins in Savannah. I worked at a fast-food restaurant there."

He waved it off. "I meant as an adult."

"I actually worked here in Dallas when I first started as an agent, and then I transferred to San Antonio. I was there until two and half years ago when my dad got sick. I came back to help take care of him." She waved away Max's look of concern. "He's fine now. Really."

"I asked you once if you'd ever move back to San Antonio, you said anything's possible. What would make you possibly want to move back or maybe even come back here?"

He'd snuck in two questions. She'd let it slide. "Would I move back to Dallas, no. San Antonio, I can't see that either, but it's funny you should bring up San Antonio again because my friend Tess—she's a real estate agent, too—just asked me to come work for her there."

"Oh?" A hint of fun faded from his gaze. "You just said you probably wouldn't move back there. Are you considering it?"

"Not really. I mean, why would I go back? I have a good job. I get to spend time with my family whenever I want to. I don't have a reason to leave. Believe it or not, I like living in Chatelaine."

He shrugged. "San Antonio is a lot more interesting."

"I have all the interesting I need in Chatelaine. I know what I want."

Max studied her a moment longer. "I bet you do."

They went back to trading questions and talked long into the night. They had different opinions. They'd experienced different things growing up. They had different preferences. He thought it was a near sin that she would choose hot chocolate over coffee, but it wasn't a deal breaker. They had some things in common, too.

They liked horses. They preferred to watch movies over binge-watching a series. They could take or leave lemonade. Over not under with a roll of toilet paper. Say no to oatmeal cookies. Say yes to chocolate cake.

They crawled into bed together tired but happy. Waking up to him in the morning was a slow rise to ecstasy.

Late that afternoon on the way back home, as the private jet reached altitude, she snuggled up to Max, resting her head on his shoulder.

He'd nailed it with his mock-mimosa toast when they'd arrived in Dallas. He had given her the perfect weekend. And in so many ways, they were a good fit.

Max took her hand and intertwined their fingers on his thigh.

Desire and happiness swelled inside of her, but so did the truth. What they shared wouldn't grow past a few perfect moments, and that was something she couldn't forget.

Chapter Fourteen

"What do you think?" Eliza lifted her arms from her sides as she glanced around the expansive empty family room.

She was showing the house to a friendly couple, Don and Nia Anders, who were newly hired supervisors at the GreatStore.

As the husband and wife looked at each other, excitement was written on Nia's face.

Outwardly, Don was reserved but interest reflected in his eyes. "There's definitely enough space down here for us and the kids."

Nia nodded. "And they'll love the pool. This is so perfect for us."

He chuckled. "Honey, shouldn't we see the rest of the house before we decide?"

Eliza sensed a sale in her future, but this wasn't the

time to push too hard or crowd their space. "All of the bedrooms are upstairs along with a standard bathroom with a shower and a spa bathroom in the primary bedroom. Feel free to look around. I'll be here if you have any questions."

As the couple walked out of the family room, Nia's low voice drifted in through the doorway. "A spa bathroom, too? Oh, Don, I love this place."

Eliza glanced out the bay window at the pool. The moment, she'd pulled into the driveway Max had come to mind. Weeks earlier, he'd looked at the same house and despite the impressive floor-to-ceiling brick fireplace in the living room, the pool, or the square footage of the bedrooms, it hadn't been right for him.

Back then, she'd encouraged him to remain patient, but a part of her had started to wonder if she could find a home that would suit his needs. And now, that morning, he was signing the closing documents at the attorney's office.

He'd asked if she was going to be there, but as the agent, she didn't have to be. And the Anders, who'd come from Corpus Christi, couldn't look at houses at any other time.

But this was also Max's moment. Yes, they'd grown closer since their trip to Dallas that past weekend. But they weren't a real couple embracing their future with a new home. This was about him achieving the dream of buying his first home. And it wasn't like they had to pretend to be together. Cal and Nancy had signed yesterday, and Max's signature was the last step in the process.

Footsteps echoed as the Anders came down the

stairs, but instead of coming back into the family room, they walked out the glass door to the pool.

Their expressions were earnest as they spoke to each other, but their relaxed body language was a good sign.

Smiling, the couple held hands.

A hint of envy pinged inside of Eliza. They were so lucky...

A vision rose in Eliza's mind, and instead of the Anders, she saw herself with Max. Happiness filled her chest as she let herself indulge in the fantasy.

Her buzzing phone pulled her from the vision, and she took it from her coat pocket. Max. He was probably calling to tell her he'd signed the papers and gotten the keys. She couldn't stop a smile as she answered. "Congratulations, Mr. New Homeowner. How does it feel?"

"Good, but..."

The lack enthusiasm in Max's tone diminished hers. "But what?"

"He and Nancy were supposed to drop off the keys this morning, but Cal changed his mind."

"What? He can't back out now. They've already signed the documents."

"Cal doesn't want to back out of the sale. He wants to hand over the keys, personally...to both of us. I know you're busy showing houses, but is there any chance you can meet around noon? If not, I understand, this is so last minute. And it's only symbolic. The Picketts fell behind in their packing so I gave them more time. I'm not moving in until the end of the week."

Outside, Nia and Don wrapped an arm around each

other's back. As he looked at her, he nodded yes. Smiling broadly, they shared a kiss.

Happiness for the couple and a longing to share a similar moment with Max prompted Eliza's answer. "I'll be there."

At the appointed time, Eliza parked behind Max's truck in Cal and Nancy's driveway.

Dressed for the office, Max got out of his vehicle to meet her. Technically, it was his house now.

She got out of the car and Max closed it behind her.

His mood was subdued. With Cal's reluctance to hand over the keys, he was probably cautious about celebrating.

"Thanks again for doing this," he said.

Striving to lighten the mood, Eliza took his hand. "I'm your totally committed fake girlfriend, remember?"

Instead of walking to the door, Max gently tugged her closer, and they faced each other. "That's the thing. You're not my committed fake girlfriend anymore. You're my real estate girlfriend who has clients to see and a very busy schedule."

"Girlfriend, huh." Eliza liked the sound of that. She couldn't stop a smile as she looked up at him. "So that would make you my boyfriend?"

"Damn right."

She liked the sound of that, too. Caught between his warmth just inches away and the cool wind at her back, Eliza gave into temptation and took a step toward him.

The front door opened, and Cal stood at the threshold. He called out with the usual impatience in his voice. "Are you two going to stand out there all day?"

Max chuckled. "Time to go."

Holding hands, they met Cal at the door.

As they crossed the threshold, Nancy joined them. She looked slightly harried. "Thanks for coming by on such short notice."

"Not a problem," Max replied.

Cal gestured inside the house. "Let's sit down. I have some things to tell you about the house."

"Oh no you don't." Nancy tone was stern, but affection was in her eyes. "You've interrupted their workday, and we have plenty to do. Just hand over the keys and let them be on their way."

Cal harrumphed in disapproval, but he reached into his front jeans pocket and took out a set of keys. He held them out to Max.

"Wait!" Eliza slipped her phone from her pocket. "Let me get a picture of this."

Cal looked at her over his glasses. "Just him? Shouldn't you be in the photo, too."

"Of course she should," Nancy expression was slightly exasperated. "I'll take the photo." As Eliza handed over the camera, the older woman glanced heavenward then smiled.

Eliza moved next Max, he held his hand out to her and she took it.

Cal cleared his throat. "Homeownership is big step." The older man took in a breath as if he was winding up for a long speech. He caught Nancy's warning look and exhaled. "I was just going to say...make sure you cherish your time together."

As Max accepted the keys from Cal, his other hand

tightened briefly around Eliza's. "Thank you, sir. We will."

"Congratulations!" Nancy beamed. "Now, smile."

As Max and Eliza looked to the older woman who was poised to take a picture, they wrapped an arm around each other. It felt natural to do it, and so did looking up at Max.

And so did the press of his lips on hers. Warm, sweet and punctuated with the gorgeous smile filling his eyes.

Eliza let herself fall into the fantasy she'd imagined earlier when she was showing the house to the Anders. That she and Max were really in this together.

"Oh, that's perfect!" Nancy said.

Max kissed Eliza again. It was perfect—a perfect daydream that one day, she'd have to let go of.

Chapter Fifteen

Moving day... It was finally here. Max let the reality of that settle in his mind.

"Are you excited?" Eliza smiled at Max from the passenger seat of his truck. She looked cute in a black hoodie, jeans and high-top tennis shoes.

Max hesitated with his confession. "Yeah, and maybe a little anxious, too." He'd checked his front jeans pocket for the keys at least a half dozen times before leaving the townhome that afternoon.

"That's understandable. And so normal. Just don't forget to pause and soak in all the moments. Today is special." Eliza laid her hand on his thigh, and for a brief second, his concentration went a little haywire.

"I'll do that." He laid his hand over hers.

The first moment he was soaking in was having Eliza with him. Except for going to work, since they'd returned from Dallas five days ago, they'd spent all their time together. It felt right to have her with him on moving day.

She glanced behind them. "I can't believe everything you're bringing to the new house is in the back of this truck and the trailer."

"Yep. New house. New furniture. I've already ordered it." He glanced in the side-view mirrors.

The tarp he'd tied down over the box in the bed of truck fluttered. The moving trailer he'd rented and hitched to the back followed straight behind.

"But I kept what was most important," he added.

"What's that?"

"The mattress and the box spring."

She laughed. "Oh, so you're planning a sleepover?"

Smiling, Max kissed the back of her hand and winked. "Something like that."

Waking up to her beside him. The experience of the first perfect sunrise from his balcony. He couldn't wait to add those two things to his collection of first moments in the house.

A few miles down the road, they could see the house in the distance. A mobile home was parked off to one side in the driveway.

Eliza sat up straighter and peered out the windshield. "Cal and Nancy are still here? I thought they were leaving early this morning."

The day they'd picked up the keys, the Picketts had confirmed they were moving today. One of their children was coming to help them finish packing and help with the drive to Fort Worth.

"Oh no, you don't think something happened with Cal. Did we miss a text?" Eliza checked her phone. "I don't see anything."

Hopefully the couple was okay.

He parked in the driveway. As they got out of the truck, Nancy came out the front door with a harried look on her face.

Before they could greet her, she laid her finger to her lips and motioned for them to follow.

Inside the house, she shut the door behind them. "I'm so sorry about this." She wrung her hands. "I know we're supposed to be gone already, but my daughter and her husband's flight was delayed, and once they landed in Corpus Christi, they had an issue renting a large enough moving truck to fit all our stuff. They didn't get here until late last night. And then Cal and I forgot to empty the shed. They're doing it now that Cal's out of the way. I finally convinced him to take a nap in the mobile home."

"It's okay," Max said, patting her arm. "Take all the time you need. I'm not in a hurry."

"Oh, thank you." Her shoulders relaxed, but she looked worn-out. "This is starting to feel like the never-ending move. We should be done in couple of hours."

"Is there anything we can do?" Eliza glanced up at him.

He was just about to ask the same thing. Max wrapped an arm around Eliza, confirming he didn't mind assisting.

Nancy's face lit up. "Are you sure you wouldn't mind?"

"Whatever you need," he replied.

"I have just a few more things in the downstairs bedroom that need to be packed up." Nancy led the way through the now vacant living room, headed toward the hallway.

The white walls had been repainted, and the rooms looked even larger without furniture.

They reached the bedroom.

An assortment of books sat stacked in a corner. Piles of framed photos were on a wood dresser against the wall. A plastic-covered mattress and box spring for at least a queen-size bed were leaned against the nearby wall with open and closed packing boxes.

"This room ended up being the catchall for the last of our things." Nancy pointed to some packing supplies on the floor. "I have protective sleeves for the fragile stuff and packing paper to wrap the books in one of the boxes. If you could tackle doing this bedroom, my son-in-law Luke can load everything up. I have to finish cleaning upstairs."

Max shook his head. "You don't have to do that. I'll take care of it."

"Oh no." Nancy picked up a blue duster from the dresser. "When I moved into this house, it was clean. And I plan to leave it that way."

He waited until Nancy was out of earshot to tell Eliza, "I really don't mind cleaning up."

Eliza brought an empty box and sleeves to the dresser. "You see how well they've taken care of this place. It's a point of pride. And cleaning the house one last time is probably giving Nancy a chance to say goodbye to it."

"I didn't think of that." He cushioned the box with paper. "This is probably an emotional day for her. They've lived here for close to forty years."

"That's a long time." Eliza slipped a picture into a protective sleeve and handed it to him. "But I get the feeling Nancy is ready to leave because of what's happening with Cal." She picked up a photo collage with oval and square cutouts within the frame. "Oh, look at this—it's them on their wedding day. They look so happy."

From the style of Cal's baby blue suit and frilly shirt, the pictures were taken around 1970. The photos showed younger versions of Cal and Nancy, but their smiles were timeless.

She held up another framed photo. "Remember how they told us they met? I bet this was taken then."

In the picture from decades ago, Nancy was dressed in fancy cowgirl gear and wore a sash proclaiming her the rodeo queen. She was smiling up at Cal who wore a cowboy hat, Western shirt, jeans and a huge grin on his face. They were clearly taken with each other.

"It really was love at first sight for them." Eliza's mouth curved upward with a soft smile. "When we had dinner with them that night, I saw this same look pass between them. All these years later, and they're still that in love with each other. It's so sweet."

The sun shone through the window, surrounding her face with an angelic-looking light that reminded him of the murals at Fortune's Castle. He couldn't take his eyes from her. Was this how Cal felt when he looked at Nancy?

Tipping up her chin with his finger, he turned Eliza's face more toward him and pressed a kiss on her lips.

She smiled at him, and his heart tripped in his chest. "What was that for?"

"I just felt like it." He gave her another quick kiss. She handed him the wrapped rodeo queen photo, and he carefully packed the picture in the box with the rest of them.

What Nancy and Cal had—how did it develop and stay so strong and not disappear after fifty years? Why had it evaporated between his parents in less than ten?

The answers escaped him, though he pondered the questions for a while.

As they were packing up the last of the books, the Picketts' daughter Diane arrived with her husband Luke. They were both relieved to see progress had been made.

Fiftyish, blond and petite, Diane had Cal's sharp, peering eyes but a ready smile. Luke looked around the same age. Tall, with a shaved head, he had the solid bulk of someone who spent a lot of time lifting weights.

Between the four of them, they loaded everything in the room inside a moving truck parked in the driveway.

Luke pointed his thumb at Max's trailer. "Want me to give you hand with anything?"

"I've got a mattress and box spring I need to get up the stairs."

"Let's do it."

Max looked to Eliza. "Not that you and I couldn't handle it."

"Oh, I don't mind." She playfully nudged him along. "Trust me."

Eliza and Diane headed back inside the house to help Nancy.

Luke chuckled as he and Max strode to the trailer. "She and Diane think alike. I have to tell you, we were so glad when we found out you were a solid buyer. With Cal's criteria, we were afraid selling the house was going take forever."

Max unlocked the padlock on the trailer. "I'm just glad he was willing to sell it to me."

"I can see why he agreed to bend the rules. You and Eliza fit well as couple. Taking care of a house in a remote area like this, you need that strong connection. You have to work together."

"Thanks." Max raised the door on the trailer. Luke's genuine praise raised a hint of guilt. But Nancy knew the truth. That mattered. And so did the good that came out of giving Cal and Nancy the freedom to leave.

When they returned to the driveway, Cal was walking slowly down the stairs of the mobile home. "I slept too long. Someone should have woken me up. We still got the shed to do."

"All done," Luke said. "Everything's already in the truck."

"Are you sure?" Cal asked. "I had some tools in a box underneath the work bench."

"I think we got everything."

Cal peered over his glasses. "Think? I better go check myself." He flicked his hand toward them. "Come with me."

Luke stepped forward.

"Not you." Cal jabbed a finger toward Max. "Him.

I'm leaving the UTV behind. I need to tell you about it." He opened the smaller door of the three-car garage.

The utility terrain vehicle—a larger, more powerful cousin of an ATV, built more for work than recreation—sat inside.

Max checked it out. It had all the extras and looked almost brand-new. "Are you sure you want to leave it?"

"No use for it in the suburbs." Cal climbed in the passenger seat. "You drive. Luke, tell my bride to get a move on, please. I know she wants to be thorough but we need to leave sometime today."

"Will do." As Max backed the UTV out of the garage, Luke gave him a casual salute and look of commiseration.

Max steered the vehicle to a small dirt road running perpendicular along the property.

As they rode, Cal pointed out the features of the UTV and the manual tucked in a compartment.

A short time later they arrived at a worn-down horse barn.

Cal checked the attached storage shed but didn't find any tools left behind. Hands on his hips he stared at the old, wooded double-stall structure. "It was solid back in the day. Used to be a paddock over there, but the fence rotted out and we tore it down years ago."

Max stood beside it. "That looks like a good place for it."

"It was."

In the mood to talk, Cal pointed out other areas around them, indicating where it tended to flood if it rained, suggesting where he might want to build a fence.

"And make sure you meet the neighbors," Cal added. "Nancy and I always made a point to do that. You never know when you might need a hand."

"Once Eliza and I are settled, we'll have to do that."

Cal huffed a dry chuckle. "Son, you can cut the act. You and Eliza are about as close to being a serious couple thinking about marriage as I am to winning the lottery without buying a ticket."

Caught off guard, Max grappled with what to say as a follow-up. "How long have you known?"

"I had my suspicions. There are certain things a man in a serious relationship doesn't forget—like how his significant other prefers ranch dressing on her French fries instead of ketchup."

Yeah, that was a dead giveaway. "So if you suspected, why did you sell me the house?"

"Because of Nancy. Don't get me wrong, I'd reneged after seeing your picture on that flyer for the bachelor auction. But that night I heard Nancy on the phone with Diane. She was crying because she'd finally thought we were going to be able to move on to the next phase of our lives. But I was pulling the rug out from under everything. She was worn out, and I didn't see it because I was stuck on the idea of finding the right family."

Blinking rapidly, Cal shifted his attention to the field. "Nancy means everything to me, and all I want is to see her happy. I told you communication is important as a couple, and I dropped the ball on that with the sale of this house. And I forgot the other important rule, too. Be honest, especially with yourself. I wish…" Cal paused as if he was pondering something.

He wished what? As curious as he was about it, Max respected the silence and didn't pry.

Cal looked around as if taking in his surroundings. "Treat your home and the ones you care about with love and respect, and you'll be a happy man. That's what my father told me."

Cal laid a hand on Max's shoulder and gave him a brief smile. "And he was right."

Max watched Cal walk to the utility vehicle, and appreciation for the man's stubbornness and values hit him. Rick had been less than a father, and Linc had done his best to step up as a parental figure, but Max didn't view him as dad.

Cal's kernels of wisdom were the closest he'd ever received to fatherly advice. And he'd never forget it.

He and Cal returned to the house, and a short time later, the Picketts, Diane and Luke said their goodbyes, and handshakes and hugs were exchanged.

Nancy was the last to walk away. She embraced Max and whispered, "Thank you."

Max replied, "Thank *you*, Nancy."

One thing Cal hadn't mentioned was if he'd tell her he knew the truth. Would Nancy ever confess to Cal?

He believed they would.

Max and Eliza wrapped an arm around each other as they watched the mobile home and truck turn onto the road.

A horn beep came from the mobile home. Nancy was driving.

Eliza waved. "Maybe we should give them a goodbye kiss and leave Cal with a good impression."

He knew they didn't have to, but he wouldn't pass up an opportunity to kiss Eliza. "We should." Max turned her in his arms and kissed her.

The lush warmth of her mouth ignited desire in him. It was almost as if she had cast a spell on him. Would he ever get enough of her?

They broke apart and Eliza released a slow breath. "If that didn't convince him…"

"Cal already knows." He had to tell her the truth.

"Since when?"

Max drew her closer. "Come upstairs with me and I'll tell you."

"Oh no." She slipped from his gasp and waggled her finger at him. "First we unpack the trailer. The sleepover comes later."

"Aren't you curious about when Cal found out?"

She kept walking and he followed. "It was at the restaurant. Ranch dressing instead ketchup."

"How did you know that?"

She grinned and her eyes lit up. "I didn't. You just told me."

Hours later, evening settled in.

Max was done with unpacking. He was ready for the sleepover. And to make more of those moments like she'd suggested during the drive to the house that morning. He hadn't set up the bed frame yet. They didn't need it. The mattress on top of the box spring was comfortable enough for tonight.

As Eliza unpacked clean towels from a plastic storage container and put them on a shelf, Max wrapped his arms around her from behind. He nuzzled her neck.

Laughing, she tried to squirm out of his arms. "Have you finished unpacking your boxes?"

"Yes." Max slipped one of his hands under her T-shirt. "And I think you're done for the day, too. I'm ready to take in my first moment."

"Which one?"

"You. I plan to have one in every room in this house." He cupped her breast and feathered his thumb over her nipple. With his other hand, he unfastened her jeans.

Eliza's breathing grew unsteady. "Every room?"

"Uh-huh, starting with my bedroom."

As he slid his hand down into her lace bikinis, she leaned in closer to him. "We really should wait until—" But when he glided his fingers through her sensitive folds, she lost her concentration and forgot her objection. She could only moan. "Oh, Max…"

Holding her close, he massaged and caressed her. Eliza chanting his name echoed along with her cries of pleasure. She came apart in his arms and he picked her up, carrying her to the bedroom.

In less than a minute, their clothes were piled on the floor, and they lay on the blanket covering the mattress.

Every brush of his lips and glide of his palms over her bare skin made his heart pound harder as pure desire built inside him.

Max rolled away from her. As he stared at the duffel bags and boxes, panic and frustration hit all at once. Condoms, he'd packed them. But where were they?

Eliza sat up and kissed the back of his shoulder. "My bag. Side pocket."

He found a string of them.

She had plans, and he was on board with every single one of them.

He put one on and went back to Eliza. Moments later, as he thrust deeply inside her, they both released shuddering breaths. Moving as one, they found their rhythm, steady then growing faster like the beat of his heart, until they both found release.

For Max, it was the first moment in his new house that he'd never forget.

In the darkness before dawn, Max awoke before the alarm went off on his phone, ready to capture his next moment.

He snagged a pair of sweatpants he laid on top of one of his duffel bags and left Eliza lying on the mattress, which was still on the floor. She slept peacefully under the blanket and comforter he'd dug out of a box during the night.

Downstairs in the kitchen, he found the coffee maker and mugs. Then he searched through the canvas bags of food items on the counter, finding what he needed. While the coffee maker brewed his K-Cup of choice, he heated hot chocolate in the microwave. It was from a packet. In the future, he'd have to learn to make it from scratch.

When the drinks were done, he took a sip of his coffee, then carried the mugs upstairs.

In the bedroom, outside the French doors, a sliver of yellow peeked over the horizon.

Max sat the mugs on the floor on the side of the mattress where Eliza slept. After putting on a T-shirt, he hunkered down beside her.

As he stroked a finger down her cheek, Eliza sleepily opened her eyes. "What are you doing up?"

"Making another moment. Come on."

She turned and looked toward the French doors. "It's still dark outside. Can we do it later?"

"Nope. It's an important moment—and it requires hot chocolate." He waved the cup under her nose.

"That important, huh?" Eliza laughed. "Okay, I'm in." She stretched, then tossed back the covers and got up. The hem of the T-shirt she'd borrowed from him sometime during the night fell to midthigh.

He tossed her a pair of his sweats and socks. "You'll need these. We're going out on the balcony for a sec to see the sunrise."

"So the next moment you want to make is the two of us freezing to death on the balcony?" she asked as she pulled them on.

"You won't freeze." He kissed her on the nose. "I'll keep you warm."

Moments later, they were on the balcony. Wisps of fog hovered over the ground. The breath from their mouths turned into puffs like smoke.

She stood in front of him, warming her hands on the mug of hot chocolate while he held the comforter around both of them.

He'd made a choice before coming outside. The coffee or just holding her. As much as he loved coffee, it didn't compare to having Eliza wrapped in his arms.

She lifted out her mug, and he adjusted the comforter so she should take a sip. When she was done, he cocooned it back around them.

Eliza glanced up at him. "The day of the open house you came out here and stood. Is this what you were envisioning—seeing the sunrise?" She knew him so well, sometimes it was a little scary.

"Yes. It's the main thing that sold me on this house."

She looked out. "I can see why. It's so peaceful."

Soft rays of orange and yellow slowly crept over the horizon, bringing light to the shadows, brightening the clouds to white puffs hovering in a sky that transformed from gray to dusky purple to blue.

The sun warming Max's face grew so bright he had to look away.

He glanced to Eliza. Face uplifted, she'd closed her eyes and was smiling contentedly into the light.

Soft emotions he couldn't describe wove into a thread of protectiveness that wound into an unruly ball in his chest.

Eliza looked up at him. "Was it as beautiful as you expected?"

Honestly, in that moment, he only saw her. He'd never felt so...fulfilled. The sunrise, the house, being with Eliza, right then, were like pieces of a puzzle that had suddenly snapped into place.

Max wrapped his arms around her a bit tighter and pressed a kiss to her temple. "Yes."

Honestly, it was more than he expected. Sharing the moment with her had made it a hundred times better.

Chapter Sixteen

"Say hi, Cap." Standing in her parents' four-stall barn, Eliza tilted her phone toward the golden, creamy-maned palomino looking out the top half of the dark-wood Dutch-style stall door.

"Hello, Carpathia. Hello, my beauty." Her mom waved from the little box at the bottom of Eliza's phone screen. "Do you miss your mama?"

Making time for a Wednesday morning video chat with her mom was the perfect way to start the day. Texts and phone calls were great for staying connected, but she missed seeing her mother's face.

When people saw her with Iris Henry, they said she looked just like her. But when she was with her dad, people would say she looked exactly like him, too.

One thing wasn't up for debate. She'd inherited her

mom's eyes, all the way down to her naturally long lashes.

The horse snorted and knocked Eliza's pale gray Stetson askew.

Dressed for riding, warmth and working in the barn, Eliza had on a sherpa-lined jacket, boot-cut jeans and her favorite cowboy boots.

Loosey Goosey, a brown-and-white Appaloosa in the second stall across the wide aisle, chimed in with a long whinny.

Eliza laughed and adjusted her hat back on her head. "That would be yes. And Loosey Goosey said hi, too."

"I wish I was there. I miss you all so much."

"Do you know when you're coming back yet?"

"I hate to say." Her mom sighed. "Every time I think we've come to a consensus about how to handle supply increases, the decision falls apart. The one thing we have finally agreed to is that the budget is already cut to the bone. If we take any more money away, we'll only hurt ourselves and the aid recipients." The conviction that made her mom good at her job reflected in her tone and on her face. "And that's our mission. To help people."

Eliza took a step away from the stall. "So what's the organization going to do?"

"It's all-hands-on-deck for fundraising. I have to attend three presentation meetings this week." Eliza's mom shook her head. "It still baffles my mind that we have to spend all this money wining and dining potential donors to impress them. We should just be able to host a potluck in the conference room, get to the point and let the donors write us a check."

"I'm sorry it's so frustrating. I wish I could help."

"You are, by giving Carpathia lots of love and her favorite hay cubes. Are you riding her today?"

"Yep. She and Loosey Goosey are both going out."

"Oh? Your father is riding with you this morning?"

Eliza hesitated. The whole fake dating bachelor auction debacle had been concerning for her parents. After spending the weekend with him in Dallas, she'd explained that she and Max were now a couple.

That confession had raised a few concerns. They'd wondered if things were moving too quickly between Eliza and Max. Her mom and dad had also questioned where she thought the relationship was going.

Explaining her no-strings relationship would have raised more alarm in her parents, so Eliza had simply said she didn't know yet.

Now, whenever the topic of Max came up, she could see concern and maybe a little disapproval on their faces.

But as they liked to say, she was grown. Rather than risk a debate, Eliza just stopped bringing him up in conversations with them as much as possible.

Sometimes, like now, it was unavoidable. "No, Max is coming by. He wanted to look at our barn to get ideas for the one he plans to build."

"He is?" Her mom's brow rose a fraction. "I see."

"What do you mean by 'I see'?"

"I don't mean anything."

"When you say that, there's always a meaning behind it."

"It doesn't matter. You don't see what I see when it comes to the two of you, and that's fine. You're an adult and you're free to make your own choices."

You're an adult... Eliza gave an inner eye roll. Her parents thought they were fooling her when they said things like that. It meant they thought she was making a bad decision.

Outside the open, sliding barn doors, she caught a glimpse of Max making the hike down the gravel pathway running from the side of her parents' house to the barn.

He'd put on a dark ball cap and had on a lightweight, insulated black jacket, jeans and black boots. One of his hands was tucked into his front pocket, matching his confident but relaxed stride.

"Let me guess." Her mom broke into her thoughts. "He's on his way to the barn now."

"Yes, do you want to meet him?" If her mom would just talk to Max, she'd probably change her opinion about him.

"Not today. I have to go." The smile in her mom's eyes was genuine. "Let me know how your ride went. And tell him I said hello."

"I will. Love you." She blew a kiss to her mom.

Her mom sent one back. "Love you, too. Bye."

She ended the call and met Max by the barn door.

Smiling, he wrapped her in a loose embrace. "Good morning." He leaned in to kiss her, but their hats got in the way. "Hold on." Max turned his ball cap around then tipped the brim of her hat up a little before he swooped in with a kiss that rocked her all the way down to her boots.

He leaned back and took her in from her Stetson to her boots. "You look pretty. I like this look."

Loosey Goosey snuffled.

Max tipped his head toward the stall. "Sounds like your horse agrees me with me."

"He's a sweetheart, but he's not my horse. He belongs to a family friend. He's out of the country on business, and my dad's boarding the horse while he's gone."

"Who does the other horse belong to?"

"That's Carpathia." Eliza led him inside the barn.

"That's your mom's horse, right?"

He'd remembered what she'd said that day in the castle. "Yep, this is her."

"She's a beauty just like you said." Max glanced at the empty stalls. "You don't have a horse?"

"I used to, but we sold him my freshman year of college. Back then, my parents were busy with their jobs." Eliza took a plastic baggie with hay cubes from her pocket. She gave one to Max. "And between classes and wanting to enjoy time with my friends, it grew harder for me to take care of him."

"But you're home now." Max fed the cube to Loosey Goosey, then rubbed the horse's neck.

She fed a cube to her mom's horse. "I can ride Cap whenever I want. And Loosey Goosey is here a lot. And my dad still boards horses for a few close acquaintances."

"Cap?"

"That's what I call Carpathia. Calling her Carp for short doesn't fit."

"She's too much of a lady to be called that."

"Exactly." If her mom had heard him say that, she would have approved. She'd have to tell her.

His phone chimed, and he pulled it out of his pocket. As he looked at the screen, he grinned. "The counter stools I ordered will be here tomorrow along with the furniture for the sunroom and deck. Perfect timing. My mom's coming over Sunday afternoon."

"That's nice. What are you making her for lunch?"

"I hadn't thought of that, but I guess I should. And I know exactly what I'll make. Beef stew."

"Oh." That was…different. Maybe she should suggest something a little easier to prepare for his mom's first visit? "Is there a particular reason you want to make her that?"

"The day of the open house, that's what Nancy was cooking. It reminded me that my mom used to make it."

That actually made sense. "Do you have her recipe?"

"Uh—no. I was thinking I could grab a few cans of it from GreatStore."

Beef stew from a can might be fine for a visit from Greg or maybe even his brothers. But for his mom?

Choosing her words carefully, Eliza rested her hand in the middle of his chest. "I tell you what. Why don't I make it? I can do it at my place and drop it off at your house."

"Or you could join us."

"This is a special time for you and your mom. Besides, Tess is popping by that day." Tess hadn't mentioned a reason for the visit, but knowing her friend, Eliza figured she wanted to talk to her again about joining her team.

He shrugged. "Now that I'm thinking about it, maybe it shouldn't be just my mom. I'll reach out to my brothers, too. And invite Greg. It'll be my first get-together. You can bring your parents, too."

"My mom most likely won't be back by then, and my dad doesn't go anywhere socially without her. They're a team."

"When she gets back, we'll have to plan something then." Max snagged Eliza by her front belt loops and tugged her closer. "So how 'bout it? Can we team up on making lunch at my place on Sunday?"

"Possibly. I'll talk to Tess and find out what time she plans on swinging by. Right now, we should team up on something else."

A sexy-wicked gleam lit up his eyes. "I like the sound of that. Which empty stall?"

She gave him a coy look from under her lashes. "I was thinking all of them."

"All of them? Really?" His brows shot up. "Cap and Loosey Goosey might not like us invading their turf."

"They'll be okay." Eliza slid her hands up his chest and gave him a brief, teasing kiss. "And I have lots of ideas about what we can do. Muck out the stalls. Clean the paddock. Exercise the horses."

A chuckle rumbled out of him. "Woman, you are cruel."

"I'm practical. The best way to figure out what you

need in your barn is to work in one and get your hands dirty."

"I'd rather put my dirty mind to work, but if you insist…"

"I do. We can explore my fantasies of doing it in a barn later."

"Wait. Not a *fantasy* but fanta*sies*?" Max looked happy and surprised.

Laughing, she slipped from his arms. "If you do a good job, maybe I'll tell you about them."

Max was a very good worker. He hadn't forgotten what he'd learned as a teen all those years ago working at Miller's Boarding Stable. As they worked and talked, he brainstormed what his stable could look like.

And his horsemanship was spot-on. He handled Loosey Goosey like a pro working beside her and Cap as they rode on a trail that circled her parents' property.

Afterward, sometime that afternoon, holding hands, they strolled to her cottage.

But Max stopped short of following her up the stairs to the porch.

She looked over her shoulder at him. "Don't want to come inside? You mentioned that you were thirsty."

"I am." The way he looked at her with longing in his eyes heated her skin and made her heartbeat ramp up. "But you're dirty. I'm dirty. And since you have a shower and we kind of like taking each other's clothes off, that's probably where we'll end up."

"And?"

"And your father probably won't appreciate that."

"My father won't be in the cottage with us. And news

flash, I'm a grown woman." For once she agreed with that observation.

"But you're *his* daughter. When you're at my place, your personal life isn't playing out on his doorstep. He's been peeking through the window blinds since we got here. I can only imagine what he's thinking."

She'd never imagined what her father might think if she brought a guy to her cottage because she hadn't. She'd never wanted to until Max.

Eliza came back down the stairs, and as Max held her by the waist, she laid her hands on his chest. "I'll take a shower and come by your place later."

"I'll be there." He kissed her and then whispered in her ear. "Pack an overnight bag. I plan on finding out more about your fantasies of doing it in the barn."

As Max got in his truck, she looked to the side window of her parents' house.

The gap in the blinds suddenly narrowed.

Eliza loved that Max wanted to show her father respect. But she also wished her father and mother would get to know Max.

She could easily imagine Max coming over for dinner and watching a ball game on television with her dad. And her mom, she would talk to him all day about horses and setting up the perfect barn. But none of that would happen.

The vision dissipated in subtle wave of sadness.

They probably didn't see the point in knowing Max better considering she didn't know where her their relationship was headed.

But she did. One day, she'd want more, and Max wouldn't be willing to risk a deeper relationship.

As much as she enjoyed being with Max, just like her parents, she couldn't allow herself to get too close to him. Because someday, it was all coming to an end.

Chapter Seventeen

Max came down the stairs on Sunday, following the smell of bacon. His stomach growled. In the kitchen, he encountered something better than breakfast.

Eliza wearing only his blue shirt. Her hip propped against the counter, she talked on the phone. With her hair pulled up in a high ponytail and her face free of makeup, she looked happy and carefree.

Who was she talking to?

As she shifted her stance, he couldn't stop his gaze from dropping to her silky-looking, smooth toned legs. Or from remembering how she'd wrapped them around his waist when they'd made love last night.

Max walked farther into the kitchen.

She smiled at him.

As he reached Eliza, he took hold of her waist. She moved closer, and the feel of her soft curves pressed against him immediately ignited desire. Max nuzzled the side of Eliza's neck, breathing in her scent.

"Okay… I have that," she said into the phone.

He should leave her alone and let her finish her conversation, but he couldn't resist sweeping kisses down her neck to her shoulder. Or pausing midway to gently nip and suck on a sensitive spot.

Eliza released a soft gasp. "Mom…" She sounded slightly breathless. "I think I got it. Can I call you later if I have any questions? Thanks. Love you. Bye."

She leaned in and kissed him.

Max joined in, deepening the kiss as he glided a hand up her thigh and under the hem of his shirt. He traced along the lace edge of her panties. He wanted in. Now.

She moaned into the kiss. "Beef stew…"

Her words barely penetrated the haze of desire that encircled him. "What?"

Resting her hand on his chest, she nudged him away. "If we're going to make beef stew, we have to start now."

Lunch…family… Reluctantly, he took his hand from under her shirt. His pent-up frustration fed into a kiss that left them both breathing unsteadily.

Smiling, Eliza slipped from his grasp. "Do you think you can get things started while I get dressed?"

"I'd rather help you undress."

He took a step toward her, and Eliza laughed, backing out of reach. "I'll let you do that later." She pointed to the countertop. "I already washed the vegetables. They need to be peeled and cut."

Max followed her gaze to the potatoes, carrots and

onion near a knife and two clear cutting boards on the counter. He looked back to Eliza. "Sure. But I better wait a minute or two before handling knives. I'm a little distracted."

"Have some coffee. It'll help you focus. Bacon and eggs are warming in the stove if you want some." She blew him a kiss and hurried away.

There wasn't enough coffee in the world to get his mind off making love with Eliza. Still, he poured himself a cup, chowed down on bacon and eggs, and got busy peeling vegetables.

His first party. He'd never envisioned having someone else there to help him make it happen. But strangely, right then, he couldn't imagine anyone but Eliza by his side.

So many good moments tied to the house were made better because of her. But he couldn't get used to Eliza always being there.

Like their talk during their weekend in Dallas had revealed, they had differing opinions when it came to relationships, especially long-term commitments.

Eliza believed in and ultimately wanted what her parents and Cal and Nancy had as couples.

Eventually, she'd leave him, just like Whitley had, because he couldn't give that to her.

As he thought of Eliza leaving him, a weird sense of loss pinged in his chest.

Eliza came into the kitchen wearing jeans and a pink fitted T-shirt. She was talking on his phone. "That's understandable. This was a last-minute thing. Hold on. I'll let you talk to him." She looked to Max. "It's Coop."

Pushing aside feelings he didn't understand, Max wiped his hands on a dish towel before taking the phone from Eliza. "What's up?"

"The lunch thing you're having today. I'm coming, but I might be late, and I can't stay long."

"No problem. Get here when you can. But I can't promise there'll be much left over. You know Linc and Greg love to eat." His brother Damon couldn't make it at all today.

"Eliza is saving me some."

"She is, huh?"

"Yep." Coop chuckled. "I knew you wouldn't so I went straight to the top."

Was it that obvious that Eliza was in charge? The thought of that made Max smile even harder.

While he and Coop briefly talked about horses, Max continued to peel potatoes while Eliza chopped the vegetables.

Rebuilding the horse barn and settling in at least two horses by the summer were first on his to-do list. Who better to get advice from than his ranch hand brother?

A few minutes later, Max and Coop ended the call.

Eliza glanced over at him. "Coop gave you some good news about finding the horses you want?"

"Yeah, he has a few leads."

"Good."

They continued working in tandem preparing the food. Their actions complemented each other's as he anticipated her next steps with cooking the beef, and she did the same with him in washing the dishes. They even tackled making biscuits together.

As Eliza stored the pan of cut biscuit dough to bake later, the rich savory smell of stew wafted through the kitchen.

Max wrapped his arms around her from behind. They should definitely throw more parties together. Would Eliza be good with that?

She looked over her shoulder at him. "What are you smiling about?"

He almost asked Eliza how she would feel about hosting more parties. But he was getting ahead of himself. "I'm just happy you're here."

She kissed his cheek. "I am, too."

Hours later, Max kicked back on the new deck sectional furniture he'd just set up.

The warmth from the square, tile-and-stone firepit in front of him was the perfect complement to the afternoon weather.

Greg sat in a chair on the other side of the pit. Max's tall, sandy-haired older brother Linc was next to him.

Linc's girlfriend, Remi, chatted in the sunroom with Eliza and Tess. To enable her to come to the luncheon, Eliza had arranged for her friend to meet up at Max's new place.

Earlier the women had bonded over interior decorating and plant tips during lunch. It had been comfortable and informal, just like he'd imagined, with everyone seated at the granite island enjoying bowls of stew, salad and fresh bread.

His mom was also in the sunroom, just listening. She

hadn't said much since she arrived, but she seemed to be relaxed and enjoying herself.

As Tess walked out the sunroom door and onto the back lawn, talking on her phone, Max noticed Greg's attention wander to the Realtor. When Eliza had introduced them earlier, Greg had barely been able to utter a coherent "hello." Since then he hadn't been able to keep his eyes off her or her mile-long legs encased in tight-fitting jeans.

Greg leaned in with a serious expression, looking from Linc to Max. "What do you think? Is this a good time to make my move?"

Linc offered up a casual shrug. "It's as good a time as any."

"Sure. Take your shot," Max added.

Greg took a sip of beer from his bottle, then set it on the wide, outer tiled section of the pit. As he stood, he pushed the sleeves of his gray pullover up his forearms, blew out a breath and rubbed his hands together.

As he walked across the lawn, Linc chuckled and shook his head. "He doesn't have a chance in hell with her. Why didn't you tell him?"

"Tall, pretty and unavailable is his type." Max turned to his brother. "Why didn't you set him straight?"

"Entertainment." Linc grinned. "We needed someone to laugh at since Damon and Coop aren't here."

"Yeah, I wish they could have made it." Unfortunately, Coop hadn't been able to stop in as he'd hoped. "I was looking forward to them seeing the house and talking to Coop about my plans for rebuilding the barn. I need to make a plan to invite you guys back to watch a game one weekend."

"Count me in for that. You know, I'm proud of you, little brother. You picked a great house."

"Thanks."

They clinked bottles and took a long pull of their beers.

Max looked up at the house and scanned the property. "A part of me still can't process I get to wake up here permanently. So much has changed."

"Tell me about it. From this time last year to now is a total switch for me, too."

Max voiced a question that had passed through his mind a few times. "Do you ever wonder what Wendell would think about how we're spending his money?"

"Nope." Linc downed the rest of the beer, then set his empty on the tile of the pit. "And it's not his money anymore, it's our money. We lived through some hard times without it. Now it's our turn to be happy."

Linc's gaze went to Remi. Since his brother had started dating her, he'd become calmer, more content. And they definitely were a serious couple.

Max took a sip of beer. He'd started to feel more peaceful and at ease since he'd been with Eliza. Did that mean something in the scheme of things? Along with the fact he'd miss her if things ended between them. No, not if, when.

But what if their relationship did continue? Despite their family life, Linc seemed to have something solid with Remi. Maybe he should ask him how he got past what happened with Rick and their mom.

Wait, was he really contemplating a serious conversation about relationships with his older brother? Yeah, that would feel more than just a little strange. And

Linc would probably see it as hilarious. Still, maybe he should.

Linc pointed toward the house. "Mom's getting ready to wash dishes. Do you want me to grab her?"

She didn't need to do that. "No, I got her. Do you want another beer?" Max gathered up the empty bottles.

"Maybe later." Linc stood and stretched. "Hand me the bottles. I'll put them in the bin. And then I think I'll go for a walk."

"You might need to take Greg with you."

On the lawn, Tess turned back to the sunroom, and Greg stuffed his hands in his front pockets and walked slowly back to the deck.

Linc chuckled as he accepted the bottles from Max. "Yeah, he might need to walk off the sting."

Max checked in to see if the ladies needed anything. They were fine. He collected a couple of empty glasses then went to the kitchen.

His mother stood at the sink with her hands in the soapy water.

He set what he carried on the counter. "You're my guest tonight, Mom. Why don't you go outside and relax?"

"Guest?" She chuckled. "You make it sound like this is a hotel or something."

"Mom, just let me put everything in the dishwasher. Seriously—"

She nudged him aside. "Doing dishes is kind of relaxing." She began washing a bowl. "It reminds me of how I used to wash dishes and keep an eye on you kids when you all were little."

What was that saying? Great minds think alike? He

snagged a dish towel off the counter. "That's what I thought of when I first saw this kitchen."

"I swear you guys had so much energy. Just watching you run around made me tired. If Linc hadn't been old enough to help, I don't know what I would have done. When the time comes, he'll make a good father." She glanced at the window in the breakfast nook that overlooked the deck.

Linc had changed his mind about going for a walk. He sat with Remi on the couch. She was snuggling up to his side, and he had his arm around her. They were talking to Greg who stood by the railing.

"They're really good together as a couple." His mom rinsed the bowl. "Being in sync will come in handy working at the bookstore."

The bookstore, Remi's Reads, was the business enterprise Linc and Remi were collaborating on together. They'd bought a former hardware store in town and were renovating it, hoping for a grand opening in a couple months. It had been Remi's dream. When the book department had been cut from the GreatStore where Remi worked and Linc had gotten his inheritance, he helped make it happen for her. Now they were both invested in seeing Remi's Reads come to fruition.

Max accepted a dish from her. "It will. I think they'll do well."

Women's laughter filtered in from the sunroom. Eliza leaned in while Tess checked out one of Eliza's earrings.

As he set the plate on the counter, his mom held another one out for him to dry. "Those earrings you bought Eliza really are beautiful. I overheard her telling Remi you bought them for her in Dallas?"

"Yes, I did."

And that's all he was saying on that topic. She didn't need to hear all the details. Like everyone else in town, his mom knew about the steamy kiss at the bachelor auction. And by now, she'd probably heard about him whisking Eliza off to Dallas.

"So are you and Eliza in a serious relationship?"

Max should have easily given the answer to that question, but for some reason, he got tongue-tied for a second. "We're spending time together."

"Oh, really? Spending time together is how your father and I got started. And in the very beginning of our relationship, he used to buy me gifts—not expensive ones." She vigorously scrubbed a pot. "And we went away together. He booked a motel in Corpus Christi so no one we knew would see us."

She shook her head and sighed. "I fell for him. And you know what happened after that. Commitment wasn't in his DNA. That's what he inherited from *his* father."

Was his mother comparing him to Rick? Maybe Linc and Remi were successful as a couple because that trait his mother had just described had skipped over Linc.

Unease gathered in Max's gut. Maybe he was one destined to fail at commitment just like Rick and his grandfather.

Later in the evening, everyone headed to the cars to leave, including Eliza. She and Tess were going back to the cottage for some girl-time.

She kissed him as she said goodbye. "I'll come by after work tomorrow."

"If you get here before me, just use the code to get in."

She started to walk away, then stopped and looked up at him. "You okay?"

A sense of dread Max couldn't explain needled inside him. He smoothed a strand of hair behind her ear. "I'm fine. Have a good time."

But he wasn't fine.

Spending time together is how your father and I got started...

What his mother told him about her and Rick kept playing through his mind over and over. Unable to sleep, he relit the firepit. Dressed in only a T-shirt and a pair of sweatpants, he didn't feel the cold. The outside temperature matched the dread that had shaped into bricks of truth that formed a wall of cold, hard reality he couldn't ignore or overcome.

More childhood memories loomed in Max's mind of his parents fighting. Rick walking out one day and never coming back. Of his pregnant mom staring at the door at dinner, as if willing Rick to come back home. The day the courier had delivered the divorce papers and she'd held them in her hands and cried as if her heart had been shattered.

The remembrances grew more vivid in his mind the next day.

Too sleep deprived to work, he left the office early. At home, he took off his shoes and went straight to the sectional and stretched out. He dreamed of Eliza.

That evening, Max groggily awoke with a blanket covering him. He hadn't brought it with him to the living room.

The sound of water running in the kitchen intensified his thirst and the dryness of his mouth. The savory smell of yesterday's stew filled the room.

But it no longer raised hunger, comfort or a wonderful memory.

As he breathed it in, desolation carved into his chest. Chances were back then, his mother had come home bone-tired when she'd made that meal for them. And she'd prepared it because she'd needed to make food stretch to feed all of them. While she'd stood at the sink washing dishes and keeping an eye on them, more often than not, she would have traded that moment for a chance to sit down and rest. But she didn't get that luxury because of Rick. If she hadn't met him, her life probably would have been easier. Better.

He walked to the kitchen. Eliza looked over her shoulder and smiled at him. A future scrolled through his mind of her beautiful smile fading.

"Hey, sleepyhead." Eliza took bowls from the cabinet. "I was just about to wake you up. We'd thawed out chicken for tonight, but we had enough leftovers for dinner so I heated them up instead. But there's no bread left."

Max tamped down the urge to kiss Eliza and hold her in his arms. He took a glass from the upper cabinet, went to the refrigerator and poured a glass of water. He drank most of it down in one gulp. As he watched Eliza stir the pot on the stove, it churned in his stomach.

"Tess had a good time yesterday." Eliza chuckled. "But she felt kinda bad about shooting down Greg. He's a nice guy, but he's just not her type."

"Did you and Tess talk about her job offer?"

"We did. But I told her no." Eliza transferred her attention from the pot to him. Hope was in her eyes for something he couldn't give her.

His stomach churned even more with nausea, despair…fear of Eliza growing to hate him because he'd hurt and disappointed her.

It was in his DNA.

Max swallowed hard. "You need to take the job."

"What? I don't want it. I'm happy where I am."

"If you turned Tess down because you believe there's an us in the equation, you're wrong."

Confusion covered her face. "Max, what are you saying?"

Max took a sip of water. He willed his insides to settle and did what he had to do—for both of them. He dropped the final brick into the wall of cold, hard reality and hurt her now instead of messing up her life later.

"I just want to make sure we don't get caught up in a misunderstanding with each other. We agreed to hook up for a while and we've been having fun. But I think yesterday might have muddied things up. Even my family got the wrong idea about us. We don't want our situation to get too complicated." Max forced a nonchalant shrug. "I was thinking we should come up with an end date. Maybe another week or two."

Eliza drew in a breath, almost as if she'd been hit. Hurt pooled in her eyes as hope and happiness drained from her face.

His own agony twisted inside of him. As she

searched his face, he masked it along with how much he cared about her. Hurting her now was for the best.

Eliza searched his face. He caught the flash of sorrow in her eyes before she looked away.

She raised her head high and met his gaze. "No. Let's end it now."

Chapter Eighteen

Eliza sped away from Max's house. Her heart pounded in her ears as she swiped tears from her cheeks and blinked back more as she drove home.

How had she not seen this coming? She should have sensed Max wanted to end their relationship in something he'd said or done. But there hadn't been any signs. Sure, he'd been a little preoccupied since the gathering with his family, but she'd assumed it was work related or that the experience of moving had finally caught up with him and he was just tired.

Sorrow filled her chest, and the truth swelled with it. By letting herself get so wrapped up in him, and all of the good moments they'd shared, she'd buried what Max had told her. He wasn't interested in something long term. Max had wanted a relationship for now. Not forever.

Long minutes later, Eliza arrived home. Without thinking twice about, she parked in the driveway, got out and rushed into the house.

Her dad walked out from the hallway leading to the kitchen. "Hey, Lil Bit, I thought…" As he looked into her eyes, his widened.

Eliza ran to him, and her dad caught her in a tight embrace. "Dad… I…" She was sobbing so hard she was shaking.

"Take slow breaths." He held her away from him. "Are you hurt? What's happened?"

Oh no, he was thinking the worst. Eliza did as he said and breathed. "No, I'm not injured. And neither is anyone else."

He grasped her gently by the shoulders. Caring and indulgence were in his eyes. "What's wrong?"

She wasn't wounded on the outside. And she was an adult. She'd dealt with her share of bad news and messy breakups. But the pain Eliza felt in her heart was deep, but she didn't know how to express it.

"Max and I broke up… But I'm in love with him."

Eliza paused in opening the door to leave her childhood bedroom at her parents' house where she'd been holed up for the past two days.

The night of her breakup with Max, she'd poured her heart out to her father, and he'd cradled her in his arms while she cried some more. He hadn't uttered one "I told you so" as he brought her meals and mugs of hot chocolate. But he didn't have to. She'd been foolish to think she and Max could jump from a fake relationship to a real one. A part of her honestly felt he'd believed it, too. He'd just woken up sooner to the truth.

She couldn't hate him for that or for his brutal honesty. Right now, she didn't like him one bit. But she'd never stop loving him. No matter how much it hurt.

Dull emotional pain twisted inside her. The urge to give into it and crawl back into bed was almost overwhelming. Tears threatened, but she closed her eyes, willing them back with a shaky breath. Her pity party over the breakup with Max was finished. She'd taken a shower and now she was going downstairs to join her dad for breakfast. Then she was going to her cottage to change out of the faded sweatpants and shirt she'd dug out of the dresser drawer. She'd call Reggie and let her know she could expect to see her at her desk tomorrow. And from there…she'd figure out the next step.

In the living room, the smell of pancakes, bacon and coffee wafted in the air.

As she walked down the short hallway, she pasted a smile on the face for her father before she walked through the archway. But her dad wasn't the one standing at the stove flipping pancakes.

"Mom…"

Eliza hurried over to her mother, sank into her tight embrace and took a breath. From a child, she'd always thought her mom smelled like serenity, sunshine and happiness.

After holding on a beat longer, Eliza let her go. "When did you get in?"

"A little after midnight." Her mother transferred two

golden, fluffy pancakes from the skillet to a plate on the counter. "I peeked in on you, but you were asleep."

"You should have woken me up."

"You needed the rest. You've been through an emotional ordeal." Faint shadows from too little sleep underscored the concern in her mom's eyes as she handed her the plate. "Your dad's been really worried about you, and I have, too. How are you?"

Feeling herself growing weepy, Eliza focused on pouring syrup on her pancakes from the squeeze bottle on the counter. She set down the bottle, then swiped a stray drop of syrup from the rim of her plate with her finger and sucked it away.

Flavored with sadness, it tasted bittersweet. She forced out a breezy laugh that sounded pitiful to her own ears. "I'll live."

The door to the attached laundry room opened and closed. The sound of boots hitting the floor echoed in the space.

A moment later, her father strode into the kitchen carrying a small brown cardboard box.

As he set it on one of the chairs at the kitchen table, he looked between Eliza and her mother, and his mouth curved upward in a faint but happy smile. "My two favorite women in the world in one place. My day is made. It'll be even better if I can get my hands on some fresh pancakes."

Eliza moved to give him her plate, but he waved her off as he poured a cup of coffee. "I can wait. You take those. Sit down and eat."

Needing a caffeine hit, she poured herself a cup of

coffee, too, before taking a seat across from her father at the table.

"Oh, wait." Her mom removed a pan from the oven "There's bacon."

Max loves bacon…

The thought came unbidden, and Eliza almost refused the slices her mom put on her plate.

No. Giving up on being with Max was one thing. Giving up bacon because of it—that had to be a huge "don't" in the almighty relationship handbook. She'd have to push through it.

Carrying two filled plates, her mom handed one of them to Eliza's dad and joined them at the table.

The pancakes and bacon were good. Being in the warm, homey kitchen eating breakfast with her parents, surrounded by their love, was even better.

Her mom picked up Benjamin's coffee. "So now that you have some food in your system, maybe you're ready to answer my question. How are you?" As she took a sip from the mug, she stared at Eliza over the rim.

But she'd already answered that question. "Like I said… I'll live."

Her father paused in taking a bite of his pancakes. "Not talking about it won't help."

Eliza almost denied she was avoiding anything, but her parents' direct stares stopped her. Looking down, she toyed with the bacon on her plate. "Now I understand the phrase 'feeling like your heart's been ripped out of your chest.' You were right. Getting involved with Max was the worst thing I could have done."

"Hold on." Her father held up his hand in defense. "I didn't say that exactly."

"And neither did I," her mom added. "You're making it sound like we have something against Max, and we don't. All along, we were just concerned about you getting involved in a relationship that you said was going nowhere and ending up in a place you didn't expect."

"Because I couldn't handle it. Obviously."

"No." Her father shook his head. "Because you put your whole heart into things. But lately, you've been settling for less in return—in your career and now in your relationship with Max."

"But I'm perfectly happy with my job."

A skeptical look came over her mom's face. "Content with your job, yes. But as far as your career or new experiences in life, you've been standing still."

"New experiences?" Eliza couldn't stop wry confusion from rising in her tone. "Where does what just happened with Max fit into things?"

"Into a pattern. You got involved in a relationship that you said couldn't go anywhere. You've stayed in a job that's only offering you the same."

She wasn't just a disappointment to herself but her parents, too? "So you think I'm failing at life."

Her mom quickly grasped Eliza's hand on the table. "No. Never."

Her father cleared his throat. "The one thing that I learned when I was recovering from my heart attack is that standing still comes from indecision. And indecision comes from fear. I know my heart attack scared you. And while you wanted to help your mother look after me, I think a big part of the reason you stayed was because you were afraid of losing me."

In the days after her father's heart attack, her biggest fear had been him not making it. She'd prayed so hard that it wouldn't happen. Seeing him every day was a gift she didn't want to miss.

"I…" Eliza swallowed against tightness in her throat. "Your recovery…you being here—it isn't something I take for granted."

As her dad met her gaze, his eyes grew misty. "Neither do I. I thank God every day for that. But one of the joys in my life is watching you living your own." He picked up the box from the chair and passed it to her mother.

Her mom pushed away Eliza's plate and put the box in front of her.

Up close, Eliza could see that it was faded and slightly dented on the side. Instead of taped, the edges were tucked under, keeping it shut.

From her parents' expressions, they expected her to look inside.

Eliza unfolded the edges and opened it. "My foil helmet and sword…you kept them." Her most prized possessions from her childhood fantasies with Lucy Belle when she was a courageous knight. As she laughed, tears of happy nostalgia pricked in her eyes. "Why are giving them to me now?"

Her father got up and hunkered beside her. "Because it's time for you to refill your own well. Conquer new challenges."

Eliza looked between her dad and mom. "You want me to leave?"

Her mom smiled. "We want you to spread your wings again. You can always fly home. We'll be here when you come back." She reached over and squeezed Eliza's hand.

Eliza's dad laid his hand over both of theirs. Tenderness was in his eyes. "While you're gone, I want you to figure out who and what deserves to be a part of your life. You're talented and beautiful. You weren't meant to hide who you are or stand still. Baby girl, go slay dragons."

Chapter Nineteen

Max stared at his closed office door as he listened to his new client on the phone.

Jack, who'd just turned thirty, lived in Atlanta, and was one of many from the online referral service he'd joined as a provider a month ago. He'd been assigned a group of employees from a fitness company that was now including financial advice as a benefit.

The stories of the staff were mostly the same and not uncommon. Too much debt. Not enough savings. But spending the day on the phone, keeping busy, explaining the basics of financial success was about all he could handle on a few hours of sleep.

Last night, he stayed on the couch instead of going upstairs to his bedroom. He couldn't. Eliza's presence was in the sheets and comforter they'd chosen together. The pillow beside his wasn't just a pillow. It was *her* pillow. But she wasn't lying beside him where up until five days ago, she'd fit so well.

The loss he'd wrestled with for the past five days clawed in his gut, threatening to climb its way into his chest. But she didn't belong with him. Eliza belonged in San Antonio, building a successful career and life without him.

"So that's my story," Jack said.

Max mentally rejoined the conversation. Glancing at Jack's intake form on the computer screen, he went straight to his tried-and-true advice. "The good news is the situation you're in isn't impossible to fix. You need to crush the more expensive debt like your high interest credit cards. You'll also want to get into the habit of adding regularly to your savings and not taking on any more debt."

Jack huffed a chuckle. "Let me guess—no more eating out or paying someone to clean my apartment."

"That might be part of the plan. But it could be easier if you have a goal."

"You mean something I want? That's easy. I want to win the lottery so all my problems will go away."

Is this where you tell me money can't buy happiness?
Yes, that's exactly what I'll tell you.

His conversation with Martin played through Max's mind. Back then, he hadn't believed what Martin had told him about people being more important than things or how Wendell could see having money as a curse. Now he understood. He could buy all the things he wanted with his inheritance. But it couldn't buy him what he wanted most. A relationship with Eliza.

He could try to explain that to Jack, but just like he had, Jack would see the money as the solution. And Jack hadn't come to him for that kind of advice.

Max checked the time. "Our time is almost up. Your employee benefit covers two more appointments. I can assist you in putting together a budget if you want to meet again."

Jack accepted the offer of help, and they ended by scheduling a video call for their next meeting in a couple of weeks.

As Max took out his wireless earbuds, a ding on his computer alerted him that someone had walked in the main door.

Jill was off for the day, and he didn't have any clients scheduled to come into the office see him.

He clicked to the camera view on his phone. His mom stood in front of the wood desk in the small reception area.

Curiosity and concern followed him to the door. He opened it. "Mom, hi. What are you doing here?"

Kimberly Maloney looked at the plant in a small vase she was holding. "I picked this up for you at the flea market the other day. I thought it would look nice in your kitchen."

"Thanks." Smiling, he accepted the gift. "I hope I don't kill it."

As she followed him into his office, she waved away the concern. "A lucky bamboo is one of the easiest plants to take care of. That's why I got it for you. All you have to do is add water to the vase so it doesn't dry out. And maybe rinse off the rocks inside the vase every now and then."

"Sounds easy enough."

"Oh, and give it some special plant food and fertilizer when it needs it."

"That sounds more complicated."

"Really, it's not." She sat in the chair in front of the desk. "Eliza mentioned she likes plants. If you ask her, I'm sure she'll know what to do."

As he settled into his chair, Max set the plant in front of him. He needed to get used to telling people. Now was a good time to start. "Eliza probably would know, but we're not together anymore."

He'd played the words in his mind several times in the past few days, but hearing them out loud sounded foreign and felt wrong.

"Oh?" His mom's brow rose in surprise. "But I thought... I mean the way you two were at your house, I assumed what you had with her was different."

He'd thought so, too. "If by different, you mean a long-term relationship—it wasn't possible. I ran into Reggie Vale at the Spur & Saddle Roadhouse the other day. She said Eliza had received a job offer in San Antonio she couldn't pass up. And as far as where I stood, you said it yourself. I'm a lot like Rick."

Confusion flooded his mom's face. "Like Rick? I never said that."

"The day when I had everyone over, and you and I were talking in the kitchen, you said the way that I was with Eliza reminded you of how he'd been with you."

"You were being good to her. That's what I meant."

"So was he when you two first got together. And then you said he changed."

Her eyes narrowed as she peered at him, as if her astute gaze was seeing straight through him, then she nodded. "I get it now. Because of what I said, you think you'll change, too, with Eliza?"

Max sat back in the seat. "It's not exactly a leap considering my track record with women. None of my past relationships worked out. My brothers and Greg have never stopped reminding me of that."

"But was it working with Eliza?"

Things had been great with Eliza. But how long would it have taken for their relationship to change for the worse?

Unable to face the questions and compassion in his mother's eyes, he dropped his gaze. "I care about Eliza. That's why I had to end things. I won't get in the way of her being happy."

"Max, look at me." Parental authority rang through his mother's voice and he obeyed. "The fact that you care about Eliza and her happiness makes you a better man."

"And part of being a better man is being honest with myself. I can be a good boyfriend, but I might not be capable of anything more than that."

"But do you want more with Eliza?"

An image of Cal and Nancy's photo on their wedding day flashed in his mind. It was followed by another image of the older couple smiling at each other at the Saddle & Spur as they talked about how they met.

Max closed his eyes, trying to block out the memories. One of Eliza smiling up at him replaced it. And he knew exactly how to answer his mother. "I do."

Kimberly joined him behind the desk, and Max opened his eyes.

As she stared down at him, compassion, strength and perseverance shone on her face. "I can't predict what type of husband or father you'll be, but I do know what type of son I raised. You're a good man, and you deserve a good life with a huge slice of happiness." She cupped his cheek. "I know you're afraid of failing or falling short, but that's part of life. And so is love, if you let it. Rick and I never had a chance at happiness together because he didn't love me. If you have a chance of happiness with Eliza because you love her, don't let the past rob you of your future."

Chapter Twenty

"Is this staying or going?" Eliza's mom pointed to a sealed carton on the kitchen counter of the cottage.

"Staying." Eliza tucked the rolled dish towel with silverware next to the plates in the moving box.

The apartment Tess had found for her in San Antonio had limited cabinet space. She was just taking the essentials for now. Down the road, she'd find a bigger place once she got settled into her new job.

I'm leaving... Her new reality. Her future away from Chatelaine. She was still processing it. The past few weeks had been filled with her and Max...together. And now that was over.

The ache that had settled in her chest since the breakup grew heavier, making it difficult to breathe.

Her mom wrapped an arm around Eliza's shoulders

and squeezed. "I know it's hard. But in time, you're going to be okay."

"I know."

But that morning, doubts about if she'd ever get over Max had crept in.

She'd come across the photo Nancy had taken of her and Max on the day Cal handed over the keys to the house. They'd looked so happy together.

But that day had been a fantasy. Yet, it had felt so real.

Eliza couldn't look at her mom right then. If she did, she'd start crying and she'd done enough of that. She was making the right choice by moving on with her life, and bucketloads of tears wouldn't get her to San Antonio any faster.

Swallowing hard, she focused on sealing the carton with tape. "This roll is almost out, and it's the last one."

"I think you might need a few more boxes and packing paper, too. I can make a run to GreatStore so you can keep packing. I needed to pick up some things for the house, anyway."

"Would you? That would help a lot."

"I won't be gone long." Eliza's mother gave her another brief squeeze before letting go. "When I get back, I'll make you some lunch."

Eliza almost told her she'd make herself a sandwich, but the tender look in her mother's eyes stopped her. Her mom needed to pamper her, and truthfully Eliza would miss being pampered by her parents. "Thanks, Mom."

Her mom left, and Eliza moved a couple of the packed boxes from the counter to the kitchen table. She picked up one of the flattened cartons leaning against stacked boxes next to the wall.

One more down, a lot more to go…

Max's voice floated in her thoughts along with memories of unpacking at his house. Of the two of them finding the right spot for his things. Of cooking a first meal in his kitchen and sharing it on the floor in front of the fireplace. Of the two of them making love that first night in his house.

When they'd agreed to pretend to be a couple, she'd never envisioned it growing to the point of them actually being together. If she'd known when he'd first walked into her office how things would end, would she have changed her mind about helping him find a home? Would she have refused to help Nancy with Cal just to avoid being hurt?

"Eliza?" A familiar voice called from the open front door.

Martin? What was he doing there? She hadn't seen him since visiting Fortune's Castle. How did he know where she lived? Had Max told him?

Eliza walked out of the kitchen. Weaving through large cartons in the living room, she walked over to greet him. "Martin, hello. Come in."

"Sorry for barging in on you uninvited. I saw Kimberly Maloney in town earlier, and she mentioned you were planning to move. I was hoping to talk to you."

Her dad's business address was listed. If Kimberly had mentioned he was the local farrier, Martin could have easily looked it up. That explained how he'd found her, but what did he want to talk to her about?

As Martin walked past the threshold, he glanced around. "I saw the U-Haul out front. I guess you're leaving soon?"

"First thing in the morning."

"Oh." His shoulders fell with a look so crestfallen she almost hugged him.

"Why don't we talk in the kitchen?" As she walked that way, he followed. "I'm sorry. I don't have much on hand, but I do have water and soda."

"Thank you for offering but I'm fine." Martin waited for her to sit down at the table before taking a seat. Grimness shadowed his face. "I need to talk to you about Max."

Concern spiked inside Eliza. "Has something happened to him? Is he okay?"

"Max isn't hurt physically, but he's not okay. He's just pretending to be. And he won't be again if the two of you don't fix things. From the moment I saw you two together at the castle, I could see it. You belong together. He won't be happy without you."

His conviction about her and Max belonging together was touching, but it wasn't meant to be. "You're sweet for saying that, Martin. But Max and I— It was good while we were together. But we're going in different directions."

"I know." Martin nodded and patted her hand on his arm. "You want your career and Max wants a home in Chatelaine, but that doesn't mean you couldn't make a long-distance relationship work. San Antonio isn't that far away."

"It's not just the long-distance part." Eliza gave his

arm a squeeze before slipping her hand away. "When it comes to a relationship, we…" She'd had time to think about it and face the hard truth. But confessing it to Martin was even harder. "Max and I don't want the same things. He doesn't want to be tied down to anyone. And I believe in the possibility of forever in a relationship. Max doesn't."

"No, trust me, he does." Martin scooted to the edge of the chair. "He's just too caught up in how his grandfather and father failed in their relationships. He's scared of being just like them, but he's not. He wants more. He wants to get married someday and have a family. He'll make a good husband and father. He just hasn't come to terms with that yet. But he will."

"And I want that for him. But I can't put my life on pause for him, hoping that he realizes that one day."

"I wouldn't want you to do that. And I'm sure Max doesn't want that either." Martin reached across the table and laid his hand over hers. "But when he finally gets his head on straight, please give him another chance."

The sincerity and genuine caring in his eyes prompted Eliza to smile at him. He showed more concern than Wendell Fortune or Rick Maloney ever did. Max was lucky to have him in his life. "You really care about him."

"I do. And I care about his brothers and sister. I owe it to Wendell to make sure they turn out okay. I'm invested in the Fortune Maloneys. I believe in Max, and I want the best for him." Martin took both of her hands in his. "And one of the best things he could have in his life is you. He truly cares about you. You have to know that."

Did she? The way Max ended things between them raised so many doubts she couldn't ignore.

A short time later, Eliza stood in the doorway waving to Martin as he drove away. She had a memory of him doing the same as she and Max had driven away from Fortune's Castle. That day had been typical of their relationship—happy moments and unexpected surprises that had raised hope as well as uncertainty.

No relationship was perfect. Not even her parents'. She wasn't expecting that. But as her mother and father had pointed out, she'd tried to commit halfway with Max, but when it came to relationships, she was all in. Max pushing her away had really hurt.

She wanted to embrace what Martin hoped and believed for Max. But risking her heart again with Max—she just didn't know if she could handle that.

How many times could your heart break and still keep beating?

Chapter Twenty-One

Eliza shut the door of the cottage behind her for the last time.

Darkness was just starting to give way to the sun turning the sky a watery bluish gray.

As she walked to where her mom and dad waited by her car parked next to the U-Haul, she swallowed past the lump in her throat.

But that morning wasn't their final goodbye. Her parents were driving the moving van to help with the move.

Her dad hugged her and kissed her on the cheek. "We'll be on the road shortly after noon." As her dad spoke, she could see puffs of his breath in the chilly air. "My work at the Hanson farm won't take long. We'll call you when we leave."

"Okay. When you get there, I should already have the keys to the apartment."

Her mom waited for her turn. She held Eliza in a tight embrace. "Are you sure you don't want me to ride with you?"

"No. Keep Dad company." Eliza traded cheek kisses with her mom. "He needs someone to sing to while he drives."

He winked at her mom. "My playlist is already cued up."

"Oh, no." Her mother gave him a playful eye roll.

During long trips, he sang along to old-school Motown tunes while he drove to occupy the time. He liked to sing love songs to her mother. It was sappy and cute, and her mom loved it.

A moment later, Eliza beeped the horn and waved at them as she pulled away. Driving down the road, she absorbed the silence. As much as she loved her mom's company, she'd wanted to say goodbye to Chatelaine alone. And to see the sunrise. She'd never look at one again without thinking of Max.

After Martin dropped by yesterday, she'd pondered what he'd said about not giving up on Max. She could never give up on him. She loved him. But as far as any hope of them moving forward as a couple, the next step was up to Max.

Farther down the empty two-lane road, the sun peeked over the horizon in front of her, bringing more light to the open fields on either side of the vehicle. Where others saw dust and vacancy, she would always see potential.

As the sun rose higher, Eliza flipped down the visor.

She briefly glanced away to pick up her sunglasses in the space between the cup holders in the middle console.

A dark truck blew past her, driving the other way.

Suddenly the squeal of tires echoed on the lonely road, and on a reflex, she tightened her grip on the steering wheel and looked in the side-view mirror. *Crap.* What was up with that driver?

The truck made a U-turn.

It looked familiar, but maybe she wanted it to be him so badly she was imagining things.

In a moment the truck caught up with her and the driver beeped the horn.

She looked in the rearview mirror.

It wasn't her imagination at all.

As Eliza stopped on the side of the road, the truck pulled in behind her. She got out and stood by the car.

Max stepped out of his truck and strode toward her like a man on a mission. Urgency was in his eyes. He reached Eliza and wrapped his arms around her. He released a huge breath. "I thought I was too late."

Surprise and subdued happiness ramped up her heart rate. He probably just wanted to wish her well. It wasn't like they hated each other. She hugged him back, absorbing the clean woodsy smell of his soap and cologne. His warmth. His strength. Eliza cataloged it all in her mind along with the good memories of being with him. This was the goodbye they should have had days ago.

Max brushed a kiss to her temple. "I should have come to you earlier." He leaned away and took hold of her hands. "Eliza, I was an ass, and I'm sorry. I acted like what we had together wasn't important, but it is. And I don't want things to end between us."

Hopefulness and happiness started to rise inside of Eliza. Maybe Martin was right about Max? Even if he was, that didn't give Max a pass on explaining it himself. "So why did you?"

"How I grew up, seeing how Rick treated my mom... I'm his son. And my grandfather was no better. They hurt and disappointed the people who cared about them. And held them back from being happy. I didn't want to do that to you."

"But you're not your father or your grandfather. You're you. Just because you're related to them doesn't mean you'll be just like them. You're a good man. I know that. Martin knows that, too, and if anyone has the ability to make a comparison judgment, he does."

Visibly swallowing hard, Max looked down a moment as he brushed his thumbs over the backs of her hands. Then he met her gaze. "I'm not doubting whether I'm a good man. But I do need to see myself as the man who deserves you. When I'm with you, I do. A man with a future as a husband...a father. And I only want that with you."

Emotions welled in Eliza's chest, and tears threatened to fall. "Oh, Max..."

Before she could finish, he briefly pressed his lips to hers. "Before you say anything, hear me out. I can't ask you to put your life on hold for me while I work though the baggage of my past. I want you to kick butt selling houses in San Antonio. I know you will. But will you give me…will you give us a second chance? I love you so much, Eliza."

All she felt for him tightened around her heart and squeezed. "I love you, too, Max. And what we have together—I know it's worth a second chance."

A radiant smile and the sun lit up his face as he whooped to the sky. He picked her straight up, and spun her around.

She laughed. Happiness alone made her dizzy.

Max put her down. "I have something for you." He reached into his front pocket and pulled something out of it.

A house key.

Max put it in her hand. "We'll have to figure out how our long-distance relationship will work. Traveling back and forth just won't be on you. I'll travel to San Antonio. But when you're here, my home is yours, along with everything I have."

As Eliza looked into Max's eyes, she clearly saw what "everything" meant. It included his heart.

Chapter Twenty-Two

A year later

"Are you there yet?" Tess voice came through the speakers in Eliza's car.

With the road practically to herself, Eliza sped past open fields dotted with mesquite and oak trees. A pale yellow and orange morning sun lit up the canopy of blue sky.

"Almost." She pulled ahead of the car in front of her, then settled back into the right lane.

"It already feels weird not to see you at your desk," Tess said.

"It feels the same not to be there."

For the past twelve months working with Tess, Eliza had spread her wings and honed her skills as an agent while connecting with people from all walks of life.

Some of them she now counted as friends. And in the process of helping others find their perfect spot in the world, she'd fallen even more in love with her job.

And Max.

They'd rarely spent more than a week apart with him coming to see her in San Antonio and her returning to Chatelaine. What they shared was one of the reasons why moving back felt so right. Along with another hugely important decision.

Two months ago, Reggie Vale had decided to retire. She'd wanted to leave the business in good hands and had reached out to Eliza. Her answer to Reggie had been an immediate yes. And Max had been fully supportive.

"Hey," Eliza said. "I left some of my new business cards on your desk before I left. Did you see them?"

"I'm looking at them now, and I'm envious, but in a good way. You've really captured something with that logo you designed. You'll definitely catch people's attention."

Tess's compliment brought a smile to Eliza's face, but she couldn't take all the credit. The graphic designer she'd hired had been the one who had skillfully combined the medieval flare of Fortune's Castle with a modern twist, creating the vision she'd hoped for Eliza Henry Real Estate Group.

"Well, I guess that's it then." Tess mocked disappointment. "Now that you have a killer logo with your name on it, I have no chance of luring you back." She laughed. "But seriously, I'm glad you're happy. I better go. I have a meeting in ten minutes. But we'll talk again soon. If you need anything, call me. I'm here for you."

Gratefulness expanded in Eliza's chest. Her friend wishing her well meant so much. "Thanks, Tess."

"Oh, and say hello to Max for me."

"I will."

Eliza eased down on the accelerator a tad more. The moving van with the bulk of her things had been sent last week. She was traveling light, just her and a suitcase.

A few miles later, she pulled into Max's driveway.

He opened the front door and her heart flip-flopped in her chest.

She got out of the car. This last time around, not seeing him for ten days had felt like forever.

Max's gaze stayed connected with hers, and he smiled.

Resisting the urge to rush over to him, she savored the view. He'd welcomed her plenty of times dressed in jeans and a T-shirt, but she wanted to catalog today. The moment she came home to him, permanently, and they moved to the precipice of something more.

She reached him, and Max cupped her face, delivering a tender kiss that made happiness rush through her and her toes curl.

A long moment later, they eased out of the kiss.

Max studied her face. "Hello."

The aftereffects of the kiss and his sexy smile made her breathless. "Hi."

As he stroked his hands down her arms then grasped her waist, his gaze dropped to her lips. "I really want to kiss you again."

"I really want you to kiss me again." Eliza looped her arms around his neck. Melded against him, his body heat seeped through her burgundy sweater and jeans, but it still didn't feel close enough.

Max leaned in, then paused. "I better not." He gave her waist a squeeze and let her go. "Otherwise, we won't make it to what I need to show you."

She couldn't imagine anything that could top what the look in his eyes had promised would have happened if he'd kissed her again.

"You need a coat." Max reached inside and snagged two of his jackets from the hooks in the entryway. He helped her into one of them.

"Where are we going?"

"Not far." Max took her hand and led her to the UTV on the side of the house.

He got in the driver's side, and she got into the passenger seat.

"One more thing." He took a bandanna from his pocket. "I need to blindfold you."

"Blindfold me?" What was he up to? "This sounds mysterious."

He smiled. "It's a surprise." After blindfolding her, he started the vehicle.

Eliza's excitement mounted as they dipped and bounced over the terrain. Soon, the earthy smell of hay and horses grew more pronounced.

Too easy. She knew where they were going.

Max kept driving and the smell faded.

If they weren't headed to the horse barn, where were they going?

Max stopped the UTV. "Don't get out. I'm coming to you."

Eliza shivered more from the excitement than the cold. "Max, what are you up to?"

"You'll see." His warm hands gripped hers as he helped her out of the vehicle and led her forward.

A soft whinny reached her ears.

"Is that what I think it is?"

"See for yourself." Chuckling, he slipped off the blindfold.

She blinked, adjusting to the sunlight. A small gasp escaped her. A temporary paddock was set up in the field. Inside it wasn't just any horse. Her heart leaped.

Max hugged her from behind. "Eliza, meet Lucy Belle the second."

Emotions stole words as she stared at the dappled gray horse. "Where did you find her?"

"At a ranch in Oklahoma. Do you like her?"

She and Lucy Belle II hadn't been formally introduced yet, but something inside Eliza told her they would become fast friends.

She turned and faced him. "Oh, Max, I love her."

As he stared at her, he shook his head as if making some internal decision. "I can't wait."

"Wait for what?"

Just as she went to lay her hands on his chest, Max took a knee. "More than anything in this world, I want you to be happy. I want us to be happy." He held up a diamond ring that winked in the sunlight. "Eliza, I love you. Will you be my wife?"

As Eliza looked into his gorgeous blue eyes, she saw more than a dream of a future. She saw the promise of trust and devotion and his belief in forever.

Her heart swelled with so much joy, she could barely speak. She held her left hand out to him. "Yes."

Max slipped the ring on her finger. As soon as he stood, he took her in his arms, and they shared a long kiss. As he pulled a fraction away, she could feel his smile on her lips. "Welcome home, Eliza."

* * * * *

Look for the next installment of the new continuity
The Fortunes of Texas: Hitting the Jackpot
Don't miss

Winning Her Fortune
by Heatherly Bell

On sale March 2023, wherever Harlequin
books and ebooks are sold.

And don't miss the previous titles in
The Fortunes of Texas: Hitting the Jackpot

A Fortune's Windfall
by USA TODAY *bestselling*
author Michelle Major

Available now!

Former childhood sweethearts Shelby Bien and Luke Thornburg have to work together to salvage their hometown's pride. Trouble is, getting up close and personal means all sorts of feelings return—and Shelby can't risk her heart again. Can she?

Read on for a sneak preview of
What Happens in the Air,
the first book in Michele Dunaway's new miniseries Love in the Valley.

Chapter One

Twelve years later

Sometimes you got lucky. You were in the right place at the exact right time. When the road forked, it led somewhere great.

Or you at least found somewhere you could lose yourself, Shelby decided. If only for a little while.

Today was one of those times. Shelby turned off US 61, exiting the most direct route from eastern Iowa City to Beaumont, Missouri. Watching the road, sky and GPS, she made a few sharp turns before wedging her hybrid into a safe parking spot along the gravel shoulder. Flashers on, she killed the engine and reached into the black nylon bag sitting on the passenger seat. She took out her favorite DSLR, stepped out into the September air and swung the lens upward.

Pure impulse had struck two miles back when she'd first seen the red-and-white hot-air balloon. The candy-cane-striped balloon's lower altitude indicated the pilot was searching for a safe landing spot, and as Shelby had been in the car for about three hours, she needed to stretch her legs, anyway. She'd changed course and given chase.

Besides, every photographer had a story about stumbling on fantastic, spur-of-the-moment shots, and how long had it been since she'd photographed a subject simply for no other reason than pure joy? Photographing hot-air balloons also reminded her of her childhood, and that's where she was headed. Home.

Currently ahead of schedule on a cross-country photography assignment for *Global Outdoors* magazine, she had the time to veer off course and take some spur-of-the-moment photos before she reached her parents' inn. While she wouldn't be able to visit with her parents long, whenever she was in this part of the country Shelby made sure to stop by. She'd surprise them later today by arriving a day earlier than expected.

Shelby shimmied over the rattling, black metal tube gate, then landed, hiking boots first, in a recently mowed pasture containing grazing black Angus cattle. Their meal interrupted by the whooshing sound of the pilot firing the burners and venting the crown, the animals trotted off as the balloon descended. The wicker basket bounced once but didn't tip upon touchdown—how many times had she tumbled out when the envelope began to drag? She grinned. Far too many to count. Four passengers laughed and clapped as their ride came to an end.

Shelby kept her finger on the shutter release, the camera constantly clicking as she captured the moment. She photographed the chase vehicle as it arrived—a huge diesel crew cab pulling a trailer. Following it was a smaller SUV. A farmer let both through the gate.

She'd participated in the familiar scene many times: first as an occupant riding along, then as part of the crew laying out the lines, and then as a pilot herself, able to fly both balloons and single-engine planes.

She began to close the gap to the basket, but hesitated as her viewfinder revealed the younger male passenger dropping to one knee. He opened a small velvet box and said something that made another male passenger put his hands to his cheeks before answering with a loud and resounding "yes!" Ring placed on his finger, he threw his arms around his fiancé and kissed him soundly the moment he regained footing. Then the newly engaged held out his left hand and the diamond-studded band to the applause of those standing around—the pilot, the two other passengers, who looked like his parents, the chase crew, the SUV occupants and the farmer. Someone popped a bottle of champagne. Shelby's photographer's instinct functioned with automatic muscle memory as she captured the scene.

She lowered her camera after someone raised a toast with plastic flutes. She'd show off an engagement ring and celebrate, too…if she ever found the right guy. Maybe, at thirty and continuously single, she should lower her impossible standards and date more. Then again, why? A permanent relationship wasn't in the cards—she was always traveling to the next exotic location, exactly like she'd once dreamed. Even this road trip across America meant she wouldn't return to her apartment in Seattle for another month, and then would only leave again after a few days. Her fake ficus collected so much dust she really should give it away.

Camera lowered, she introduced herself and exchanged information with the happy couple so she could send them copies of the photos. Behind them, the crew deflated the envelope, which was the part of the balloon filled with air, and unclipped the ropes. The pilot's head shot up when he heard her last name. "Bien? Any relation to John Bien of JBMT ballooning?"

"Yes," Shelby said warmly. "My father."

"Heard about your dad's broken arm. Shame he and Mike won't be flying in either of the two Missouri races coming up. Great guys. Helped me out of a jam once. Tell 'em Caleb Munson says hi."

"I'll be sure to tell them." As he walked away, Shelby frowned and returned to her vehicle. Caleb's words didn't make sense. The only thing ever grounding her dad and Mike Thornburg was an uncooperative Mother Nature. As close as brothers for the past twenty years after leaving the military, the two men had experienced unparalleled success in both their businesses and hot-air-balloon racing.

She'd find out soon enough. She planned to surprise her parents by arriving a full day early, making her standard forty-eight-hour visit almost seventy-two. As the satellite radio station blared to life with the latest pop hit, Shelby's tires crunched over loose gravel as she navigated back to the main highway.

Several hours later, nostalgia hit the moment her car began vibrating over the centuries-old bricks of Main Street that had been unearthed by the town's council twenty-three years ago. As she drove down Main, a welcome *bumpety-bump-bump* said that she was "almost there." As she passed by familiar storefronts and restaurants, the stress of the drive peeled away with every rattling jolt.

Beaumont never seemed to change—the redbrick or white quarried stone historic buildings dated back to the late 1700s, when westward explorers had used the Missouri River town as a launch point. Now each intersection allowed for a view down the cross street to the slow-moving river.

She opened the driver's window, letting in mid-September air that contained a hint of pending fall. She'd stayed in Seattle following college, a logical choice as *Global Outdoors* could quickly send her abroad from Sea-Tac airport to anywhere, from Asia to New York. But no matter how far and wide she'd traveled, visiting Beaumont meant returning to familiarity and roots.

Shelby inhaled a deep, humid breath, and with it, a pungent whiff of the hickory smoke from Miller's Grill—Mr. Miller made the best barbeque found anywhere, especially the brisket and pulled pork.

Another mandatory stop was Auntie Jayne's Cookies. A rare curbside spot beckoned, and Shelby parallel parked. She climbed the small flight of stairs and a bell jangled over the royal blue painted door. The elderly woman behind the counter lifted her head and stopped reading *People* magazine. "Shelby? What a surprise!"

Shelby grinned. "It will be. My parents are expecting me tomorrow."

"They'll be delighted." Jayne James wiped her hands on her blue gingham apron. "Let me look at you. I don't think I've seen you since for what, four years? Normally my daughter Zoe's here."

Mrs. James gave Shelby a once-over and Shelby endured the scrutiny. A late bloomer, her last growth spurt had been the summer following high school, when she'd topped out at five-nine. Shelby reached up to ensure the ponytail holder remained in place. If not, her dark hair would fall to her shoulders.

"What can I get you? Chocolate chip still your favorite?"

Shelby grinned. "You know it. I'll take three dozen assorted with extra emphasis on the chocolate chips." Shelby checked her silver explorer watch, which confirmed she'd arrived in plenty of time for the inn's afternoon tea service.

Mrs. James snagged a square of waxed paper from the pop-up box and handed Shelby a chocolate-chip cookie, which looked like a delicious sombrero because of the extra scoop of dough on top. "See if they're as good as you remember."

Shelby bit into the edge, and sweet brown-sugar flavor made her taste buds do a happy dance. Shelby waved the cookie before taking another bite. "This is delicious. Better than the finest Paris macaron."

Mrs. James brushed away the compliment and busied herself with loading cookies into a white paper box. "Snickerdoodles, your second favorite if my memory serves."

Mrs. James's memory could give an elephant a run for his money. Nothing on Main Street ever got past her. "Yes, but better give me some oatmeal raisin, sprinkle and sugar cookies so there's a nice variety," Shelby said. "Ooh, and some of those chocolate ones with the white chips."

"Will do. So have you seen Luke yet? He's moved back."

She hid her surprise and dismay by nibbling the cookie. "No. I didn't know he was in town."

Her parents hadn't said anything. Were they afraid if she found out he'd moved home she'd find some excuse to skip even the shortest visit? As she had so many times before?

Thankfully Mrs. James didn't notice Shelby's discomfort and instead was starting to fill cookie boxes. "You two were always off on some adventure. I remember how you both would run down that sidewalk after church as fast your little legs could carry you, trying to see who could reach the door first. You look as if you could beat him now."

"Uh, thanks." A daily workout regimen kept her in top shape, a requirement for the physicality of her job. It still bothered her that altitude sickness had kept her from leaving base camp and summiting Everest. She'd prepped a year for that.

"Such a terrible tragedy about Maren. To lose her like that. She was your best friend, wasn't she?"

Trying not to bristle, Shelby kept her tone even as she set the record straight. "No, she moved here in November. We hung out a few times after Luke went to London, but then I left for Wyoming."

"Oh, that's right. The contest."

"Yes." The prize for winning a national photo contest—which the photographer at the inn had told her about—had been a three-month field experience. Slightly jealous of Luke's adventures in Europe, which he'd told her about in full detail in early correspondence, photography had helped ease the emptiness. He hadn't been at her locker between class. He hadn't sat next to her at lunch and swiped her French fries. He hadn't helped her with her AP Chemistry homework. Losing her other half had made her feel adrift. Was that why she'd allowed Maren into her headspace, let her sow the seeds of doubt? Then Shelby entered and won…and when Luke returned from Europe, Shelby had been in Cheyenne.

Maren had been waiting in Beaumont.

And all these years later there was little point in telling Mrs. James how a lifetime of friendship and love between Luke and Shelby had disappeared in an instant following a huge, long-distance fight. College and internships, and then her job, had kept her busy and far from home.

She'd been asleep in the Serengeti when Luke and Maren had announced their engagement on Christmas Eve. At a weather station in Antarctica when they'd married in a small ceremony in Cincinnati, where Maren and Luke had lived following college. The top of Machu Picchu when their daughter was born. Deep in the depths of the Amazon when Maren had passed from a fast-acting cancer two years ago—Shelby hadn't even known Maren had been sick. By the time she'd returned to civilization, her parents had signed her name to the flowers, card and donation, and sent her the obituary notice in one of their emails.

Her parents knew her work came first. She'd already achieved milestones—she was the youngest photographer at *Global Outdoors* and its only full-time female. With other magazines fighting to survive and cutting permanent staff in favor of using freelancers, Shelby knew her job could be here today and gone tomorrow should *Global Outdoors* follow suit. Hard work, not luck, had kept her in the game.

Not that Shelby regretted winning the contest. Childhood dreams were for children and she'd grown up. Life was best lived being in the present.

Cookie devoured, Shelby wiped her lips with a brown paper napkin and put it and the wax paper in the trash can. A colorful flyer advertised the weekend's fall festival. "Dad told me the inn's booked."

Mrs. James loaded oatmeal raisins next. "The festival will be busy. You caught me in a rare moment of calm. Are you staying long?"

"Until Monday morning. I figured I'd take photos of *Playgroup*, too. They usually fly the weekend before the state race."

Mrs. James paused midway through filling the last box. "Then you don't know."

The unsettlement Shelby experienced in the Iowa farm field returned. "Know what? My dad won't let a broken arm keep him from a practice. Even if he misses the state race next weekend, the town one's the weekend after. Plenty of time."

Mrs. James's face wove into concerned lines. "Oh, dear. He and Mike aren't speaking, much less flying. The town sponsorship is in limbo for both weekends."

"What?" Frowning, Shelby passed over her credit card, but Mrs. James waved away the plastic with a flick of her hand.

"Consider these a welcome-home gift. Or a bribe. Maybe it's good you're here. Maybe you can talk some sense into your dad. We've all tried and failed. Do you still fly?"

She did, but... A wrinkle deepened between Shelby's eyebrows. While Mrs. James's words helped clarify what Caleb Munson meant this morning, Shelby didn't understand how two lifelong best friends weren't speaking, much less racing. Then again, look at her and Luke. "My parents didn't say anything."

Mrs. James pushed the filled boxes a few inches in Shelby's direction. "I'm sure they didn't want to worry you. Been almost two months since your dad and Mike spoke to each other. And that was yelling."

"They've worked through issues before." Surely during the course of forty years there had been some disagreements between her dad and Luke's father, right?

"Not this time. You know the run-down bar on North Main?"

"Yeah." Attracting mostly college kids, Caldwell's could get rowdy depending on the band playing. However, it was an institution.

"Last January the new city-council members took office, including your dad."

Shelby knew this. She'd celebrated her dad's November win via video call, as she'd been in Singapore.

Mrs. James didn't miss a beat. "Mike bought Caldwell's in February. In March, the council decided North Main should be family friendly and passed an ordinance requiring liquor sales be less than fifty percent of an establishment's total revenue. The law went into effect July first and forced Caldwell's to close, same as two other places."

Shelby absorbed the ramifications. "Mike's a real-estate developer. He'd hate to have an investment lose revenue."

"Exactly. Your dad was the deciding vote. So Mike's threatened to sue if your dad touches the balloon."

Shelby could picture Mr. Thornburg's anger at having to close a profitable bar. Her dad could also be stubborn, especially if he thought he was working in the town's best interests. "Sounds complicated."

"Neither will back down and it's far too late for the city to sponsor another balloon. We'll have no balloon in our own race. We're sick over it. It's embarrassing."

Mrs. James shuddered as if she'd had a visible chill. "The entry fees for the state race are nonrefundable. Mike insisted your dad reimburse the town and your dad refused. They've always represented Beaumont. We want our balloon and our best friends back. Try, will you?"

Beaumont was a close-knit community, and Shelby imagined everyone felt caught in the middle. Perhaps that was another reason why her parents hadn't told her any of this. Or about Luke's homecoming. Shelby stacked the three boxes onto her arm, shaking her head at Mrs. James's offer of a shopping bag.

"I don't know what I can do. I'll try. But no promises."

Mrs. James picked up her magazine and fanned herself. "Missouri mules and fools, both of those men. You make any progress and I'll give you free cookies for life."

"I'll talk to Dad." *And* figure out why he hadn't told her. "I can't believe he or Mr. Thornburg would deliberately hurt the town's reputation."

"Those two were the reasons we started our race. People come from all over the country. How can we host it and not have our own entry?"

With a sympathetic smile, Shelby turned for the door, the cookie boxes now balanced in both arms from chest to chin. The doorbell jangled, and Shelby paused. She peered around the stack so she didn't plow into the incoming customers.

A curly-haired brunette girl whose hair had been tamed into pigtails raced into the store about the same time as an arm covered in soft dark hairs pushed the door inward and held it fully open. "I beat you fair and square!" the child squealed with delight.

Déjà vu washed over Shelby. While the hand was twelve years older, the shape remained similar. She recognized the faded scar on the forearm—she'd caused it when she'd accidentally crashed her bike into his.

"Mrs. James, I won! I finally won!" Realizing someone else was standing in the store, the girl gazed at Shelby with an expectant anticipation. Shelby noted the child had Maren's perky bow lips and Luke's deep brown eyes.

"Hi," Shelby said, her feet rooted as the six-foot frame of Luke Thornburg stepped inside. Her photographer's eye assessed him. He'd filled out—like her, he'd aged and lost his gangly teen awkwardness—but the same dark blond hair swooped away from his forehead. His face registered a mixture of shock and surprise, and his full eyebrows lifted.

They'd once been so in sync, and she knew her expression mirrored his, complete with the small O shape her lips made. She closed her mouth and schooled her features into a neutral expression, a requirement for someone who saw life through the camera lens—observing the action but not taking part.

"Shelby." Luke's mouth formed her name as if more than a decade hadn't passed, and a sliver of bittersweet longing for lost dreams stabbed into her heart. She ignored the pulse of adrenaline running in her veins.

She'd been in far trickier situations, like dangling off a cliff in the Front Range of the Rockies, but those instances hadn't involved facing her former best friend and first lover—the one who'd declared in emails he wanted to marry you.

Until he hadn't.

"Luke." They stood almost eye to eye and Shelby drank him in. His chambray, button-down shirt was tucked easily into the waistband of his leather-belted jeans, the rolled-up sleeves of the shirt the epitome of casual fall fashion.

He noticed her midnight blue highlights. "I like the hair."

"Dad?" Anna—that was her name, Shelby's parents had sent her a scan of the birth announcement six years ago—tugged on Luke's hand. Her emotions a roller coaster, Shelby was grateful for the interruption.

"Let's get you a cookie, sweetie." Mrs. James led Luke's daughter toward the display case. "What's your pleasure? I made giant sprinkle cookies this morning and I know how much you love them."

Unlike Anna, Luke didn't move. Instead, his brow creased and he studied her in that thoughtful way he always had, as if he could peer inside her soul and see something no one else could. The idea he might still be able to sense her deepest secrets bothered Shelby, and she held the boxes aloft as a shield.

"You look well, Shelby."

"So do you." The truth slipped out—where was the age-thirty dad-bod flab? Why couldn't his blond locks be thinning, his hairline receding? But no. He looked as gorgeous and fit as ever. She'd have to maneuver past him to reach the door, and escape was a necessity. "Got to go—good seeing you. Haven't even made it home yet. We'll catch up later."

Breezy, friendly words, said like "How are you?" with no expectation of any real answer.

Luke's gaze pinned her like an arrow hitting the bull's-eye. "Promise?"

"I gave up pinkie swears." As the barb hit home, he frowned, and she stepped purposely toward the exit. "I'll be busy with Dad. I'm leaving Monday. Must get these there before tea. Nice seeing you."

"Shelby—"

A myriad stream of emotions—everything from sadness to anger to longing and desire—threatened to burst forth and betray her. She always imagined their next meeting being something she could control. She'd be calm. Sophisticated. Flick her hair as if she didn't have a care in the world. Not appear road-worn and carrying cookies. And there was no point in rehashing the past, not when she'd load up her car and drive away Monday morning. She cut their conversation short with a "Got to go. Enjoy your cookies!"

She tried to sweep past him, but because the store was tiny and its few tables were strategically placed against the wall, the layout forced Shelby close enough to smell his aftershave—sage with a hint of sandalwood and musk, so very him. Once she'd run across a similar fragrance in a market in Marrakech, and it had made her think of him and the childhood friendship they'd lost by believing they could make it more.

She'd left the market and headed back to her hotel, where she'd used the action of sending photos to her editor as a way to put both the market and Luke in the rearview mirror. Later, when Shelby had climbed on a flight for Lake Victoria and the Kenyan shoreline that evening, she pretended she'd left it all behind.

But clearly, she hadn't.

Today, the queen of leaving fled the cookie shop at a nonchalant pace. She balanced the boxes like precious cargo as she waited for a car to pass before crossing over the brick cobblestones, leaving behind wonderful aromas of baked goods and Luke. She refused to look back.

As a newer version of the same model car he'd ridden shotgun in throughout high school drove away, Luke forced himself to turn from the window. Shelby was back. A short visit—not quite four full days—but after years of never expecting to see her again, running into her at the cookie store had caught him by complete surprise. It was also clear she couldn't wait to get away from him.

He didn't blame her, despite her actions being a punch to his gut.

Luke exhaled deeply and watched Anna pick out cookies. Despite Shelby's longer hair, now streaked with blue, he'd recognize her anywhere—same oval face with the pretty smile. Same bright hazel eyes with some flecks of gold. Same tug on his heart. She'd been his best friend, closest confidante and love of his life. Now they were worse than strangers.

Luke shook away the disquieting thought and focused on his daughter, the best thing to come from his and Maren's marriage. Anna excitedly pointed at this and that, and when Mrs. James caught his eye, she passed no judgment on Luke's encounter with Shelby.

Instead, she went back to helping Anna with the task of picking out six different cookies.

"I see you chose a sprinkle one," he said as Anna finally decided on her half dozen.

Anna pointed to the case, where trays of cookies beckoned. "I also got a snickerdoodle, and a chocolate-chip—that's for you—and a fudge brownie one, a peanut-butter one for Grandpa and a sugar cookie for Grandma."

"They'll love you for thinking of them." That was his daughter, the kindest and sweetest person he knew and someone who always thought of others first. The other day she'd given out stickers to everyone in her kindergarten class "just because."

"I put together an assortment for Shelby, too." Mrs. James folded the bag so the top closed. "She hadn't heard about the fight."

"No?" He'd been living with the fallout.

Mrs. James handed the bag to Luke, who dangled the edges between his fingers. "I told her the town hopes your dad and John work through this. *Playgroup* needs to fly. I asked her if she still flew, but she didn't answer."

Luke knew Shelby would never let any certifications expire. Not after working so hard to get them.

"I like balloons," Anna interrupted. She had crumbs stuck on her lips, and Luke removed a napkin from the silver dispenser, handed it to her and pointed to her face. Anna dabbed until Luke's nod told her she'd wiped off all the cookie particles. "Remember, Dad? The fair lady twisted a turtle bracelet from a green one."

"Not those kinds of balloons," Luke corrected gently as he handed Mrs. James a ten-dollar bill. "The ones that go up in the air. Like Grandpa's. Like the time we went to the balloon glow. Remember how all the balloons were lit up like Chinese lanterns?"

"Ooh, those were pretty," Anna said. "Are we going again?"

"Of course." Even if *Playgroup* wasn't there.

Mrs. James handed Luke his change. "So is your festival booth ready to set up?"

Luke put the coins in the pocket. "Yes. But our booth and theirs won't be side by side like before. A quilter or something is between." He turned to his daughter. "You ready, Anna Banana?" He moved toward the door.

"Last one there's a rotten egg," Anna called.

"Not this time." He didn't feel like racing. Not after seeing Shelby.

"Aw, Dad," Anna protested.

"Do you want me to crumble the cookies?" A better excuse than reminding her that a few seconds ago she'd protested she was "too big." She'd already grown and changed, developing daily into her own independent young person.

Hearing Anna's "no," Luke winked at Mrs. James and held the door open for his daughter. "Let's go."

They stepped outside and began to walk to his parents' house so she could deliver the cookies. It took two seconds before Anna began skipping her way down the brick sidewalk and pulling ahead of him.

Rather than calling her back, he admired her verve and energy. She'd been three when Maren died. To give Anna as much of a normal childhood as possible following the loss of her mom, Luke had remained in their home in Cincinnati, near Maren's parents. Anna knew her mommy was in heaven and missed her, but his daughter was proof of resilience and the power of new memories. Anna was growing up, ready to grasp the brass ring with both hands. When Maren's parents had announced they were moving to Florida, Luke had used the opportunity to return to Beaumont on August first. So far, Anna loved Luke's hometown. She'd even led him through her kindergarten classroom during open house a few weeks ago, introducing him to the new friends she chattered about constantly. He watched as she bounded ahead, knowing the way, asserting some independence yet still safe with her dad right behind her.

She'd reached the wrought iron fence surrounding the postage-stamp lawn of the Blanchette Inn, and as Luke passed by, habit had him glancing at the wide front porch. He noted that the ever-present, large green wreaths adorning the polished-wood, double front doors were displaying hot-air-balloon ornaments. Mrs. Bien made each month's wreath herself, and long ago he and Shelby had helped.

Habit meant Luke craned his neck toward the third-floor balcony. How many times had Shelby and he sat up there cross-legged? They'd watched the tourists walk by below, counted the boats out on the river and talked of all their hopes and dreams. To this day Luke couldn't pinpoint why he'd listened to Maren. What made him not recognize the snake in the garden until far too late?

By then, though, her illness and Anna had kept him with her. He couldn't bear to be separated from his daughter, and he never would have tried to take her from her mother.

Moving to Beaumont was a second chance. A do-over of sorts.

And now he'd seen Shelby and everything that had happened, all the anguish and mistakes, had come rushing back.

The inn behind them, Anna bounced through the open gate of the next brick building and ran up the sidewalk leading to the large three-story Federal-style house where Luke had grown up. While his dad had acquired an extensive real-estate portfolio of houses and commercial buildings, his mother liked living on Main Street, next to her best friend.

The front two rooms of the first floor also held Luke's mom's business. Wall shelves filled with home-made specialty soaps and body scrubs lined the perimeter. Specialty candles and other products his mom accepted on consignment could be found on the round tables scattered throughout. He noticed a new display of pumpkin-scented candles, which would be a top seller during October.

Anna retrieved the bag from him and rushed her way up to the counter. "Grandma, I brought you a cookie!"

Luke followed leisurely, watching as his mom finished ringing up a customer before giving Anna her full attention. She bent to give her granddaughter a hug and squealed over how sugar cookies were her favorite. She took a big bite and said, "Yummy. Thank you." And then she added, "Do you have homework?"

Anna shook her head enough to make Luke dizzy. "No. We're off tomorrow because of the festival."

"Really?" Luke's mom arched an eyebrow. "You're not pulling my leg?"

"Uh-uh." Anna's curly pigtails jiggled as she laughed. "But don't worry. I will read. We checked out books at the school library today and I got two chapter books."

"Chapter books already. My, my."

Anna nodded. "They aren't big chapters, but that's okay because I can figure them out. Mrs. Lewis says I'm a good reader."

"Yes, you are." The bell tinkled as the customer left the shop. His mom gestured with her partially eaten cookie and pointed to the bag in Anna's possession. "Why don't you take these cookies in to Grandpa? I bet he's hungry. You did bring him one, didn't you?"

"Of course. I would never forget Grandpa. Grandpa," Anna called, disappearing through the doorway behind the counter and into the family section of the house.

Luke picked up a bar of his mother's famous lemon-scented soap. He felt rather than saw his mother tilt her head—she was studying him, as if she knew something was wrong. How did mothers do that? "I haven't seen that look since you were little and thought you saw Casper," she said. "What's wrong?"

Luke bristled with mock indignation. "Hey, the apparition was real. This building is well over two hundred years old. Something paranormal could have made that stuff fall off the shelf."

She shook her head. "While other buildings on this street are haunted, this one's not. You had the stuff too close to the edge and overloaded it. So let's concentrate on the look on your face. Something's up."

"We have a lot to do before the festival opens at four tomorrow." That was safe. But the next part wasn't. "And Dad's feud. How's it all going to work?"

His mom wiped her hands on her ruffled apron. "Same as always. Lots of arts and crafts being showcased, fireworks tomorrow and Saturday night, and good food and entertainment all weekend. If the weatherman is to be believed, perfect weather. That means tourists and money to be made. Your dad will be civil or he'll answer to me, if that's what you're trying to get at."

Luke nodded. The entire length of South Main Street would become a pedestrian byway of booths, one of which included his mom's wares. In addition to the tourists staying at the inn and other B and Bs, the event would draw visitors from miles around.

She swiveled the credit-card machine. "I sense there's more, but I suppose that'll do for now. Stay for dinner. I've made enough beef Stroganoff to feed an army. Your sister's coming by, too. So it'll be family time."

"Okay, but we have to go home first."

"You should have moved in here, since you're here enough."

Luke had considered the idea briefly when he'd decided to return, but as he was used to having his own space, he'd politely rejected the offer. "Nah. You keep your sewing room. The apartment is perfect and Joe's Art Gallery downstairs is a quiet neighbor."

"Well, it's far better than living over that bar. If I'd known the drama that place would cause." His mom frowned as she made reference to Luke's first plan, which had been to claim the small apartment over Caldwell's. But the upstairs required a gut rehab, same as the bar area itself. Closing the place had been inevitable, not that his father would admit it. Still, his dad had given him carte blanche on the reno project, leaving it up to Luke to find a business plan the city would approve. "Mrs. James brought up the fact *Playgroup* is still grounded."

His mom sighed. "She means well and I'm doing my best. But your father is a proud man with a vacant building bleeding money. It might take him experiencing the consequences of not racing before he comes around."

Luke raked a hand through his hair. "That's too late. We have to do something now."

His mom straightened some brochures stacked on the counter. "I've already given your father my opinion. If you have an idea, take it up with him."

"I will." A group of customers entered and Luke welcomed the opportunity to follow in Anna's footsteps. But something made him pause in the doorway, and then, even though he'd sworn to himself he wouldn't say anything, he dropped his real bombshell. "By the way, Shelby's back in town for the weekend. I ran into her in the cookie store."

His mother's expression instantly softened. "Oh, Luke. Are you all right?"

No. Luke shrugged off the hurt. "It's fine. We were civil. She looks good, though. Really good."

The bell jangled, and another group of customers walked in. As his mother turned to greet them, Luke made his escape.

Chapter Two

Fewer than two minutes after leaving the cookie store, Shelby parked in an empty spot marked "resident," directly under the welcome shade of a 200-year-old oak tree.

Her parents' inn was an early 1800s structure—the stones forming the exterior walls and fireplaces had been chiseled by slave hands and carted to location by mule. Determined to remember and honor those whose forced labor had created the inn, her family had installed a marker on the inn's front lawn. Her dad had also tracked down descendants, who now held a family reunion every three years at the inn with all expenses paid. Beaumont had gone further by renaming some streets, paying reparations, installing a permanent exhibit at city hall and creating a scholarship fund. The town felt it was the least it could do.

Shelby stepped out and stretched. Even though it was too early for the oak to display any hints of the blazing reds, oranges and golds it showcased each October, the huge canopy provided nostalgic welcome. When she'd been in kindergarten—Anna's age—she and Luke used to build huge leaf piles and jump into them, scattering the leaves around only to rake them again and repeat the whole process.

Shelby shut the driver's door using the bottom of her foot—the cookie boxes filled both hands and her camera bag fit into the familiar dent in her shoulder. She'd retrieve her luggage later. Her mother's herb garden lined the back brick walkway—the large, round knee-high pots contained basil, mint, sage, tarragon and lemon balm. Each spring her mom put out the green-colored ceramic pots, and she'd store them once the growing season ended.

The walkway also wove through her mom's flower gardens, until the path through the deep back lot forked. One direction went around the side of the building to the front entrance the guests used. But Shelby climbed the back stairs to the wooden screened porch, where wind chimes tinkled in sporadic breeze. She elbowed the back doorbell. Her mom came into view, flicked the lace curtain and immediately threw open the door.

"Surprise!" Shelby greeted.

"Shelby! You're a day early! Oh, my goodness." Her mom set down the laundry basket, took the cookie boxes from Shelby's hands and set them on top of the towels. Then she drew Shelby in for a huge hug. As long as she could remember, her mother always smelled like roses, and today didn't disappoint.

"It's my body lotion," her mom had once told a five-year-old Shelby. For the next two years, Shelby had to have her own bottle, until she'd reached second grade and required more independence.

In her teens, she had worn the smelly designer-knockoff perfumes and used the latest, trendy shampoo in an attempt to be cool. How naive she'd been. Now comfortable in her skin, Shelby used whatever the hotel stocked. It all worked, even if not as well as the soaps Mrs. Thornburg made.

The rose-scented hug worked its magic and the final vestiges of stress fled. To this day, Shelby hadn't found or experienced a better floral scent anywhere in the world.

They stepped apart and Shelby received a thorough once-over. "I swear every single time you come home you've changed. This time it's your hair. Are those colored highlights? They're fabulous."

"Midnight blue." Shelby held out the end of her ponytail so her mom could examine it. "I did this when I was in London. I mean, why not? It's subtle and just at the ends. Like it?"

"Yes. Yes, I do," her mom admitted with a laugh. "It looks great. I saw a girl at the supermarket and she was totally purple. Should I do something different?"

Except for hints of gray, her mom's hair was the same as in the wedding photo hanging in the third-floor hallway. "Don't change a thing. You're perfect the way you are." Shelby meant every word. "Is Dad here? I can't wait to see him."

Her mom tucked a stray strand behind her right ear. "He's out. The doctor might have his arm in a cast, but he refuses to sit still. He had some council meeting up at city hall, so Anthony drove him."

Anthony was their family's handyman. In his sixties, he'd been with the inn for thirty years. More than an employee, he'd become part of their family.

Based on what she'd learned at the cookie store, Shelby decided not to ask what her dad was doing at city hall. "I stopped for cookies. I figured you could serve them for tea. Some for us and some for the guests."

"We're definitely having a good year reservation-wise. The guests will love them. Thank you."

"You know me. I love sweets and I had a craving." Shelby set her camera bag on the kitchen counter. She reached into the cupboard for a tall glass, then filled it with water from the sink faucet and drank while her mom retrieved a serving platter. "I ate one already. Considering going back for number two." Shelby snagged a snickerdoodle. "Which I'll do now."

Her mom chuckled as Shelby bit into the cinnamon-flavored cookie and expressed a gastric "mmm" of delight.

"So good. Have one." Shelby gestured toward a box.

"Maybe later. Even looking at Jayne's cookies makes the pounds go straight to my hips."

"Mine, too, so I'll run on the Katy Trail tomorrow. And by the way, you look great." Her mom had a few more lines on her face than in the wedding photo, but looked fabulous. Even though she never stayed long, Shelby tried to see her parents at least once every three months.

Her mom moved chocolate-chip cookies to a serving platter. "You know I've tried to make them like this. While I know how Jayne James gets this extra scoop of batter on top, I can't seem to duplicate it."

"At least she can't make your coconut pie or your mile-high lemon meringue. Even I can't. My meringue falls every time." Shelby washed down the last of the cookie with sips of water. One nice thing about being home, Beaumont had some of the nation's best tap water. Shelby'd been in places where she hadn't dared to drink the water.

"If you stay long enough, I'll show you the secret." Her mom clasped her hands together in delight. "Thank you for surprising us. I'm so happy you made it in time for the start of the festival. We're gonna have so much fun."

"I can't believe how big it's gotten."

Shelby leaned her hip against the counter and snagged a third cookie. Delicious peanut-butter flavor hit her tongue. "The sleepy festival I remember now closes down the streets."

"It's really taken off these past two years. Whatever you do, don't spoil your dinner."

Shelby relished her mom's familiar chiding. "Trust me, I'll still be hungry. I skipped lunch in favor of some snack crackers I ate in the car."

Her mom appeared concerned. "Should I make you something? A sandwich?"

"No, no. These cookies will hold me."

Her mom didn't appear convinced. "Let me know if you change your mind. I plan to spoil you with food so good you'll never leave."

But Shelby would go, despite her parents' wishes otherwise. Pushing aside a twinge of guilt, she switched subjects. "I heard about Dad and Mr. Thornburg from Mrs. James. Why didn't you tell me?"

Her mom sighed. "I figured it would be over by now. You know about the ordinance?"

Shelby nodded.

Her mom twisted her hands into her apron. "It's a mess. Mike took your dad's vote personally."

"But Dad was doing what was right."

"In his mind, yes. Cynthia and I don't know what to do. It's not like they haven't had fights before. They'll stew for a week, figure it out and things go back to normal. It's like blowing off steam. This one's different. Mike feels betrayed and your father won't back down because he'll lose face."

"I'm sorry."

"Me, too. We were at Miller's shortly after Caldwell's shut its doors, and when they passed each other in the hallway..." Her mom shuddered. "We didn't want to worry you."

"You also forgot to mention Luke moved back. I ran into him in the store."

Her mom appeared sheepish, confirming she'd deliberately kept Shelby in the dark. "You weren't here and the feud kept me distracted."

Shelby let the excuse slide. Besides, she and Luke

were ancient history, even if seeing him had made her heart miss a beat. "You and Mrs. Thornburg are okay, right?"

Her mom finished transferring the cookies and stored the rest. "Yes."

"After I take some pictures, I can help with the booth."

"Is your luggage still in the car?"

"Yeah. I'll get it now. Unless you need help?"

"I've got them. All the guests are checked in, the strawberry tarts for tomorrow's breakfast are baked and your dad and I made reservations for tonight. Call Miller's and tell them to change it to three people."

Shelby's mouth watered. "I can do that."

Her mom washed and dried her hands. "Perfect. I'm so glad you came for an extra day."

"Me, too." Shelby kissed her mom's cheek. She knew it was hard on them to have their only child living so far away. "I love you and it's good to be home."

"We love you, too. It's not the same, flying to wherever you are, even though I loved Hawaii."

Once, after she'd finished an assignment to photograph scientists who studied volcanoes, Shelby had flown her parents out for a two-week vacation and tons of quality time in paradise.

"If you're sure you don't need me to do anything," Shelby offered again.

"No," her mom insisted. "Go unpack and don't forget to call Miller's."

After lifting the platter, her mom entered the inn's front parlors and Shelby heard the oohs and aahs of guests. Shelby returned to her car and removed the trash from today's drive. She carried two handfuls to the community dumpster located in the alley.

She was struggling with the heavy lid when a hand shot out and helped. "I see we had the same idea," Luke said.

"Thanks." She tossed in her items, and he followed with a white garbage bag. The heavy plastic lid thudded closed and reverberated. Luke stepped back and shoved his hands into his jeans. Shelby quickly jerked her gaze to his face.

"Everyone like the cookies?" he asked.

When he smiled, emotions long buried flared to life. Longing surfaced. She worked to keep her tone light. Neutral. "The guests were making appreciative noises when I came out for my luggage."

"That's great."

He fell into step beside her as if it hadn't been years since they'd walked side by side. Shelby decided she had two options. Be bitchy and add to the family feud, or be civil and neighborly and try to put the past behind her. Perhaps after this weekend, and after their dads stopped fighting, it wouldn't be so awkward if she came home for the holidays, something she'd purposely avoided.

As for the fact that he smelled divine and strode beside her like he belonged—irrelevant. The days when he'd been her whole world were long gone.

She lifted the tailgate, but Luke beat her to her luggage. His firm fingers wrapped around the handle. He set the suitcase on the concrete pad and made sure the wheels didn't start rolling before he grabbed the second, larger bag. "This it?"

"Yes. Normally I travel lighter, but I've been on the road for two months."

"You always said you planned to travel. I guess you got your wish. Where were you this time?"

"Stateside. I was in the Dakotas. Minnesota and Iowa."

"Your parents told mine how much they miss you. Proud of you, but missing you."

Shelby shoved aside the guilt. "Speaking of parents, I can't believe our dads aren't friends."

Luke closed the hatchback and the trunk clicked. "We thought we'd be friends forever."

"True." She frowned. How dare he bring up their long-ago friendship? Especially as he'd been the one to end it by betraying her.

She dismissed their experience. "We were kids. They're adults. And what about *Playgroup*?"

Luke lifted her cases and carried them toward the house. "My dad told me, and I quote, he's 'not flying with that man.' He's dug in."

"They've been friends forty years. All this over having to serve more food?"

"It's a bit more," Luke said.

They reached the bench underneath the old oak tree. Shelby pointed. "I have a few minutes. Tell me." She sat on the wrought iron and patted the spot next to her. She ignored the familiarity of the movement. How many times had she asked Luke to sit with her here?

Luke set her suitcases next to her and sat on the opposite end, his knees about a foot away. Long fingers rubbed the tops of jean-covered thighs, calling attention to how fit he was. "I always said I wanted to run my own business."

He had. "Which is why I was surprised when my parents told me you became a lawyer."

"Was a lawyer," he corrected, and Shelby experienced a surprised jolt. "I left that behind when I left Ohio. Do you ever remember me dreaming of being a lawyer?"

"It's been so long," Shelby hedged, knowing the answer was no. At age six, he'd been the one to help her with her lemonade stand—they'd raised over one hundred dollars for charity after he'd taken over. She'd made the lemonade and popcorn—he'd built the stand and done the marketing and selling.

"I believe we declared we'd live forever side by side, with me running my mom's shop and you running the inn."

The memory created twinges of regret. "We were kids with silly kid dreams." She waved her hand as if shooing away a fly. "And you were always terrible at making soap."

"Still am," Luke admitted with a rueful laugh. "My sister's taking over. Maren's father was a lawyer, and it seemed like a natural path."

"It's logical you'd work to make her happy." Shelby pushed aside the bitterness. His betrayal shouldn't still resonate, but it did. She'd loved him with all her heart. But they weren't meant to be. If they had been, they wouldn't have fallen apart so quickly. Maybe seeing him this weekend would finally allow her to fully let go.

"After Maren died, I did some self-assessment." Luke

fidgeted on the bench and rubbed the top of the denim covering his thigh. "I missed Beaumont. This is home. My dad bought Caldwell's for me."

Her forehead creased. "You wanted to own a bar?"

"No. But I wanted to come home. Now the bar's closing because of the new city ordinance and it has accelerated the timeline of my figuring things out. A closed building is not an asset. You can hear my dad saying that, can't you?" His lips puckered wryly and he shrugged.

"I can." She watched as a monarch butterfly flitted and landed on the full-bloom dahlias to the right of the bench. Seemingly without a care in the world, the creature opened and closed its wings. "I'm sorry."

He jerked a hand through his hair, something he'd always done when exasperated. "You don't need to apologize. You have nothing to be sorry for. And I hate that you and I aren't friends."

The butterfly flew off and Shelby's nerves heightened. He wasn't talking about Caldwell's. "We're different people in different worlds. What's important is mending the rift between our dads."

"I'd like us to be friends as well."

Shelby stretched her fingers. To her impressionable heart, Luke's rejection had stung. He'd started dating Maren when Shelby had been in Wyoming. But for him to not tell her—to hear it from Maren, of all people… "I know it sounds harsh, but I'm leaving in a few days. We don't have to rehash what once was when the future results will be the same. I don't live here anymore. You do."

She was no longer a small-town teenager dealing with the high of a huge, wondrous new love and the crashing anguish of heartbreak. Even if she felt like a flittering butterfly when around Luke, any relationship, even one as simple as being friends, was doomed to the same time and distance issues as before.

"My job is fulfilling and I love traveling," she continued, perhaps to convince herself as much as him. "Mastering the camera freed me to find myself and see the world."

In essence, photography had provided Shelby the perfect escape, and she'd run fast and far away.

Luke clasped his hands. Released them. "I liked the story you did on the blind climber who was bungee jumping into all the great gorges."

She'd conquered one of her greatest fears by jumping into one of the gorges herself. "That was a fun assignment. I've met so many interesting people." But she never stayed. She entered their orbit and cycled out. His words sunk in. "You followed my career?"

"We were friends. Despite what happened, it didn't mean I wasn't interested in your success. You followed your dreams."

Once, he'd been her dream. A raw, uncomfortable twinge brought doubts to the surface. Many times, in the early days, she'd caught herself ready to contact Luke and share her latest adventures. Then she would remember how Maren had called her to apologize for seducing Luke. Shelby had told Maren she'd forgiven her—a lie. There was more, but Shelby refused to relive it. She'd managed to keep Luke and her hometown firmly in the rearview mirror. She was a big-city girl now. Happy.

She stood abruptly, bumping into her luggage. "I'll see if there's anything I can do on my end to soften my dad. But I know he won't back down from doing his job."

"Okay. Fair." Luke leaned forward, but remained seated. "I've been working on a new business plan and hope to get the permits soon. That might help."

Asking about his project would signal interest, and she refused to tumble down the rabbit hole. "Even if you reopen, someone has to fly *Playgroup* two weekends from now."

His gaze locked on to hers. "What about you?"

A flutter of panic mixed with excitement and Shelby took a step back. "I'm not flying *Playgroup*." Although she could. She'd passed her biennial flight review within the last nine months, since her photography work often took her up in the air for shots drones couldn't get.

"Why not? You've flown her before."

Where had he gotten this idea? *Mrs. James*. Shelby inhaled a calming breath. "That doesn't mean I should do it now."

He rose. "Give me a good reason you can't. You pilot. I'll crew. We can leave our dads out of it. Come on, Shelby. It's for the town. Our families. My daughter. The common good. The entry fee is already paid. What do you say? One more L-and-S adventure before you go jetting off again?"

L&S Adventures. Her mom had photo albums full of them. The volumes sat on a shelf upstairs.

A long pause, bordering on awkward, ensued. She

couldn't get involved with him. Already she sensed a spark, a flicker of chemistry. Neither could be allowed to ignite. "I sympathize, but I didn't come here to fly."

Although a deep-down impulse urged her to do just that, to experience the rush of controlling a hot-air balloon. She loved being up in the sky, floating over the landscape while the heat from the burners mixed with the cooler air surrounding the basket.

"When's your next assignment?"

"A month away. But I'm driving back to Seattle with a few planned stops along the way to finish my current series."

"So there's nothing calling you back immediately? No cat? Boyfriend?"

She thought of her dusty ficus. "No. But I haven't seen my apartment in forever."

He reached for her but dropped his hand. "You probably don't even have food in your fridge."

Busted. She cleaned out the appliance before each trip, not that it ever contained anything more substantial than take-out containers or frozen meals.

"Work with me," Luke urged. "Stay. We can fly together. Saving the town? That'll be a bonus."

When she hesitated, he said, "We have a few practices, stand the balloon up at the glow, race and save the town pride. You go home being a hero and you'll spend extra time with your parents, which will make them happy. You'll still have two weeks to drive back. I have access to *Playgroup*. What do you say?"

Luke could sell ice in the frozen tundra. His wicked and engaging smile had always convinced her to participate in each and every one of his seemingly hare-brained schemes, which, 99.9 percent of the time, had not only worked out well, but had also far exceeded their wildest expectations. The man had more good ideas up his sleeve than common sense, which he also had in spades.

She grabbed the handles of her rolling suitcases. "I've got to get inside."

Luke nodded, the movement swift and easy. "I'll touch base with you tomorrow. You know Anna's ready to pull some plastic ducks out of your family's duck pond."

Luke strode off. Shelby remained rooted. Her photographer's eye caught everything. He didn't lumber or shuffle, or step gawkily as if he had a rock in his shoe. Nor did he move stealthily like a cat or bound over the pavement like an excited puppy. He had the fluidity of a calm stream on a relaxing fall day. She sighed.

Despite how he'd destroyed her, he remained the standard by which she judged all other men. She pivoted, and behind her, she heard the clang of the metal latch of the gate in the privacy fence between their properties as it opened and closed.

"There you are," her mom said as Shelby brought her luggage inside. If her mom had seen Shelby sitting outside with Luke, she thankfully didn't bring it up.

"Do I have time for a short nap?" Shelby asked, suddenly drained.

"Of course. Dinner's at seven."

Shelby glanced at her watch. "Perfect."

She opened the dumbwaiter, set her luggage inside,

sent everything up to the third floor and took the back stairs two at a time while making the phone call to Miller's.

"Of course," Mrs. Miller told her, "we have room and can't wait to see you. It's been too long."

Shelby shoved her phone into her pocket, retrieved her luggage and carried it to a bedroom that had remained almost unchanged as the day she'd first left. While the antique canopy double bed had a new comforter, the tiny rosebud wallpaper was as old as she was. Framed prints of her photographs covered spots where posters once hung. She approached the 200-plus-year-old fireplace, which had been converted to gas in the 1990s. Her favorite stuffed animal sat in the middle of an ornate mantel covered with decorative trinkets. She lifted the lid of the Swiss-chalet music box she'd purchased in one of Main Street's antique shops. The waterwheel in the lower right began turning and the tinkling notes of "Edelweiss" burst forth. Seven notes in, she snapped the lid closed. Luke had convinced her to save up and buy it, and even after everything that had happened, and how it reminded her of him, she loved the box too much to give it away.

The corner of the mattress gave as she perched on the edge. She caught her reflection in the oval mirror attached to the white vanity, part of the bedroom set that had been her Christmas present at age five. Then, she'd believed fairy tales came true. Luke was a prince and she a princess. A tomboy princess, but a princess nonetheless.

Then she'd learned *Grimms' Fairy Tales* were actually a series of dark concoctions meant to scare and terrorize children. She rose and went to her closet. She tugged on the metal chain to turn on the overhead light, and reached up to grab a small lockbox. She set the carved wooden box on the bedspread. Went to her camera bag and removed a key chain. The smallest key fit the lock. The black hinges sprang open, and Shelby dug under a few papers to remove a rubber-banded stack of photos. She flipped through them, finally finding a specific set. She fanned out the pictures of the balloon race the fall of her senior year of high school. *Playgroup* had won, to the town's delight.

Everyone looked so happy. There was the photo of the group inflating the envelope and another launching *Playgroup* into the air. Another one was of the entire group posing with the trophy. Yet another was of her and Luke mugging for the camera. She remembered the day and the participant dinner vividly, for it was the night she and Luke had slow-danced romantically for the first time. He'd held her tightly in his arms, her head nestled against his chest. Later, he'd asked her to be his girlfriend and go to homecoming with him. Three words summed up the night in her memory: Best. Night. Ever.

She fingered the photo showing her with her brown hair up in a ponytail, retainer in her mouth on full display in her big smile. By Christmas, she'd only had to wear the retainer at night. Back before spring of senior year, she'd never cared about appearances because she and Luke had been geeky together.

She stared at Luke's image. No, he was never geeky. Tall, relaxed, popular, kind and handsome were all better descriptors. They'd been each other's firsts in so many things. She sighed. He could have provided closure by telling her he wanted to see other people, or that his feelings had changed. His cheating had made the breakup even worse.

She picked up another photo and studied the happy faces of her parents and the Thornburgs. Over the years she'd seen even more victory pictures like these. Now, unless she piloted the balloon, their families wouldn't even participate. Disappointing everyone seemed so wrong.

She'd missed out on so much these past twelve years—a loss that was more acute whenever she returned home. Was that why she never stayed long? Was remaining on the road her way of proving she didn't miss Beaumont and the memories it contained?

As for Luke, why did her heart still give a little jump, as if it skipped a beat? She'd experienced more than a flutter of interest. She could be forgiven for not being immune to how well he'd aged. Thirty had nothing on him except for making him an attractive man.

Like old times, she'd sat on the bench with him. Wistfulness for the past, she decided. That was all this onset of melancholy was. She picked up the picture of her and Luke and their families. Luke's sister, Lisa, was in the shot with her husband, Carl. They'd been newlyweds for not even a month, choosing to marry a few weekends before the fall festival.

She had never fully explained why she'd avoided Luke, simply telling her parents they'd chosen different things and broken up. She'd hidden her true feelings by going straight from her summer photo experience to Seattle for college, and her parents had brought her belongings to her. Luke had followed Maren to Ohio. When Shelby visited Beaumont, by tacit, unspoken agreement, her mom and dad kept her up-to-date on the life of their best friends' son but they never levied an opinion or pried. They'd trusted her. Believed in her goals and supported her. Figured she'd tell them when she was ready, and since she didn't visit that much, they also didn't want to scare her away. Hence why they hadn't told her the latest, that he was back.

Boba, the inn's resident blue point Siamese cat, entered, weaving her way through furniture legs before rubbing her face against the smaller suitcase. The five-year-old cat hopped on the bed, kneaded the blanket and settled down for a nap. Shelby scratched Boba behind her soft gray ears, eliciting a brief purr. Then Shelby took one last look at the photo.

If she piloted the balloon, maybe she'd prove to herself—once and for all—she wasn't carrying some ridiculous childhood torch for a man who'd cared so little. She'd be able to rip off the fantasy blinders of Luke as being her soul mate—the reason all other men she met paled in comparison. She'd *truly* move on.

She locked the photographs away, returned the box to the closet and turned out the light. Too keyed up, she walked to the third-floor balcony and stepped out.

Late-afternoon sun from behind the inn cast shadows on the street below. Visible over the tops of the buildings across the street, the sun made the Missouri River shimmer in ever-changing hues.

She heard a girl's shout and saw Anna skip out the front gate of her grandparents' house as she yelled, "Race you home!"

Luke, following leisurely, called out, "Don't get too far ahead," and they turned and went south, down the brick sidewalk until they disappeared from view under a thick canopy of tree branches still covered with leaves.

They didn't live next door? Shelby curled her fingers around the railing as something tugged deep inside her heart. The church bell chimed five, and down below, Main Street shops began to close. Sadie Hall came out of the bookstore and brought a rolling cart inside; she owned the shop with her mom. Mrs. Coil retrieved the chalkboard sign advertising twenty percent off the jewelry in her shop. Mr. Collins watered his petunias in the two planters outside the double front door of the haberdashery. Shelby noted everything had changed, and yet somehow stayed the same. Nostalgia tugged, and some of the earlier tension she'd washed off during her mom's big hug crept back, arriving with a push-pull of swirling emotions Shelby didn't trust herself to decipher.

Despite the above-average heat, she shivered, so she went back inside, climbed into bed and drew the covers up to her nose. Shelby couldn't risk her heart. Not again. She wasn't going to fly *Playgroup*, not when doing so would put her into close proximity to Luke. He and the town would have to come up with something else.

* * * * *

Don't miss
What Happens in the Air
by Michele Dunaway

Available February 2023 wherever
Harlequin® Special Edition
books and ebooks are sold.

www.Harlequin.com

#2965 FOR THE RANCHER'S BABY
Men of the West • by Stella Bagwell

Maggie Malone traveled to Stone Creek Ranch to celebrate her best friend's wedding—not fall in love herself! But ranch foreman Cordell Hollister is too charming and handsome to resist! When their fling ends with a pregnancy, will a marriage of convenience be enough for the besotted bride-to-be?

#2966 HOMETOWN REUNION
Bravo Family Ties • by Christine Rimmer

Sixteen years ago, Hunter Bartley left town to seek fame and fortune. Now the TV star is back, eager to reconnect with the woman he left behind...and the love he could never forget. But can JoBeth Bravo trust love a second time when she won't leave and he can never stay?

#2967 WINNING HER FORTUNE
The Fortunes of Texas: Hitting the Jackpot • by Heatherly Bell

Alana Searle's plan for one last hurrah before her secret pregnancy is exposed has gone awry! Her winning bachelor-auction date is *not* with one of the straitlaced Maloney brothers but with bad boy Cooper Fortune Maloney himself. What if her unexpected valentine is daddy material after all?

#2968 THE LAWMAN'S SURPRISE
Top Dog Dude Ranch • by Catherine Mann

Charlotte Pace is already overwhelmed with her massive landscaping job and caring for her teenage brother. Having Sheriff Declan Winslow's baby is just *too much*! But Declan isn't ready to let the stubborn, independent beauty forget their fling...nor the future they could have together.

#2969 SECOND TAKE AT LOVE
Small Town Secrets • by Nina Crespo

Widow Myles Alexander wants to renovate and sell his late wife's farmhouse—not be the subject of a Hollywood documentary. But down-to-earth director Holland Ainsley evokes long-buried feelings, and soon he questions everything he thought love could be. Until drama follows her to town, threatening to ruin everything...

#2970 THE BEST MAN'S PROBLEM
The Navarros • by Sera Taíno

Rafael Navarro thrives on routines and control. Until his sister recruits him to help best man Etienne Galois with her upcoming nuptials. Spontaneous and adventurous, Etienne seems custom-made to trigger Rafi's annoyance...and attraction. Can he face his surfacing feelings before their wedding partnership ends in disaster?

HARLEQUIN
PLUS

Try the best multimedia subscription service for romance readers like you!

Read, Watch and Play.

Experience the easiest way to get the romance content you crave.

Start your **FREE TRIAL** at
www.harlequinplus.com/freetrial.